# *An* Intriguing Proposition

## DEFIANT HEARTS PREQUEL

# Sydney Jane Baily

cat whisker press
Massachusetts

Copyright © 2014, 2022 Sydney Jane Baily

All rights reserved under International
and Pan-American Copyright Conventions.

Published by **cat whisker press**

Cover: Philip Ré
Book Design: **cat whisker studio**
Editor: Chloe Bearuski

ISBN-13: 978-1957421032

# DEDICATION

To my dearest friend
**Marliss E. Melton**
You've been with me every step of the way.
I honestly don't think I could have, or would have,
published my first book without your support.

*Love you.*

# OTHER WORKS

## The RAKES ON THE RUN Series

Last Dance in London
Pursued in Paris
Banished to Brighton
Gretna Green by Sunset

## The RARE CONFECTIONERY Series

The Duchess of Chocolate
The Toffee Heiress
My Lady Marzipan

## The DEFIANT HEARTS Series

An Improper Situation
An Irresistible Temptation
An Inescapable Attraction
An Inconceivable Deception
An Intriguing Proposition
An Impassioned Redemption

## The BEASTLY LORDS Series

Lord Despair
Lord Anguish
Lord Vile
Lord Darkness
Lord Misery
Lord Wrath
Eleanor

## PRESENTING LADY GUS

A Georgian-Era Novella

# ACKNOWLEDGMENTS

I want to thank my beta readers—Toni Young and PTPR. This was a better story because of your input. And I offer my undying gratitude to my editor, Chloe Bearuski, who as usual infused my writing with her grace and composure.

# PROLOGUE

"Father," Elise said, after tapping on the door, which was already slightly ajar. Family meant everything to Oliver Malloy, and his wife or any of his four children knew they were always welcome to enter his study.

He looked up from the paper he was perusing.

"Yes, sweetcake?"

*Sweetcake*—the nickname for a child. Yet at twenty-one years of age, Elise was a child no longer. Today, she wanted to ask him a particularly delicate favor, perhaps the hardest thing she'd ever done. Her stomach clenched with apprehension.

"Are you terribly busy?" she stalled as her heart raced.

"Never too busy for you." He removed his glasses and gave her his full attention.

Walking around her father's paper-strewn desk, Elise leaned against the edge of it, looking down at his intelligent, kind face.

"Remember that man we met today?"

He wrinkled his nose while thinking, a habit her youngest sister, Rose, shared as well.

"A number of men crossed our path today." Smiling gently, he cocked his head, once full of dark hair that was now mostly gray. "Which one?"

"At the bank, Father. You remember? The tall one with the coffee-colored hair and thoughtful hazel eyes."

Her father's eyebrows shot up while his eyes widened. "Oh! . . . *Hm.* Let me think. Hazel eyes, brown hair. The handsome young one, correct?" He couldn't help teasing her.

She blushed and nodded.

"You're interested in him, I take it."

She loved that he got directly to the point. Shyly, she nodded again. "Would you find out if he is attached?"

Her father looked at her with his inky-blue eyes so like her own. Reaching out, he patted her hand. "I'm glad you're not still grieving over young Randall."

The mention of her dear friend who had passed from consumption two summers earlier even now elicited a wave of loneliness. They'd grown up side-by-side as next-door neighbors, played together, learned to read from the same primers, ridden horses, and shared their dreams. It had been widely assumed they would eventually declare a love match and marry. Her mind wandered to his fair hair and blue eyes. She'd been very fond of Randall, but she'd never loved him.

"First, we need to know his name," her father said. "I don't believe I recall—

Her thoughts snapped back to the present. "His name is Mr. Bradley," she told her father softly. "Michael Bradley."

# CHAPTER ONE

*Two Years Later*

Elise stared down at the letter from the Massachusetts National Bank, sucking on her lower lip and considering. Even now, her first instinct on seeing the missive had been to run to her father. Naturally, this would have been his responsibility were he still alive.

Her thoughts flickered next to her younger brother. However, she was loath to bother him. She knew Reed had been strained over the past few years, and not only by taking over as head of the family. A couple years prior to that, the girl he'd loved had fled the country in the wake of a particularly nasty scandal.

*Good riddance,* Elise thought, having never liked the vain and shallow Celia.

Of course, Reed had willingly and effectively taken up the mantle of family patriarch after their father's untimely death a year earlier. Oliver Malloy's shockingly sudden passing after a brief illness had left them all reeling. While her brother had supported their mother with compassion and strength, he'd also set up his own law practice, and taken over not only his father's clients but the unenviable role of trying to keep his sisters safely out of harm's way.

Currently, Reed was knee-deep in a high-profile trial that seemed to be going terribly wrong, while at the same time, he was considered by all of Boston to be the smart young lawyer who could make everything right. He would be traveling to Portland, Maine, the very next day to depose a witness.

Elise fingered the thick cream-colored paper from the bank. Yes, Reed had enough on his sterling silver plate.

Her mother, Evelyn, who had sunk into a seclusion of deep grief from which she was only now emerging, was clearly overwhelmed by Elise's younger sisters. Sophie's latest desire to go overseas to study music had met with a lukewarm reaction from their mother, although Elise thought it was the best thing for her sister. Sophie, already an accomplished pianist, would definitely rise to the occasion and needed only to get Reed on her side to make it happen.

Naturally, their mother worried about losing sight of any of her daughters, most especially the youngest, Rose, a talkative pixie and an incorrigible imp, who was never beyond doing something impetuous.

Elise sighed. *What to do?* She could probably handle whatever the matter by herself.

With a sense of foreboding, she broke the seal, opened the missive, and scanned it. However, she barely took in its meaning before the name at the bottom leaped off the page: *Michael Bradley.*

The letter could have come from any other officer of the bank, but it hadn't. It had come from *him*, and it brought back her humiliation as if it were yesterday. Her father's discreet enquiry into Mr. Bradley's social situation had turned up the unwanted news that he was, in fact, seeing a woman, someone she vaguely knew by name. If that had been the end of it, it would have been nothing more than a minor misplacement of her curiosity.

However, someone with a loose tongue had wagged it unforgivably into the young banker's ear. The next time she saw Michael Bradley while waiting at the courthouse for Reed to take her to lunch, the man had ambushed her like a fox on a hen. In the middle of broad daylight, Mr. Bradley had approached her across the vast expanse of the lobby. Her welcoming smile froze and then died as, to Elise's intense mortification, he thanked her for her interest in him.

*Her interest in him!* Good God, she'd nearly died on the spot.

She still remembered the feeling of being unable to breathe while cool moisture seemed to break out all over her. Complete and utter humiliation. If he'd been a gentleman, he wouldn't have put her through it, but rather, he would have pretended to know nothing about the situation. If anything at all, he should have only vaguely smiled and nodded in her direction when he saw her.

He'd even expressed an apology—an apology for what, she had no idea! She'd felt sorry for the young lady with whom he was involved, if he was going to go around expressing regret over said involvement. And the whole time, he had a smile on his face as if thoroughly pleased with himself.

*Cocky bastard,* she had thought to herself at the time.

Highly unappealing and again, not very gentlemanly. She'd barely stammered a useless denial when luckily, her brother had arrived to escort her to lunch. She'd been unable even to return Mr. Bradley's expression of good will and good day.

It had taken her a week to leave the house without ducking her head, imagining everyone was snickering at her behind their gloves and parasols. *The girl who'd asked after Michael Bradley.*

She'd waited another year before going into the bank again, and that time, it was to accompany her mother after her father died. She'd made sure to stay well clear of the man's office and was grateful not to see hide nor hair of him.

Suddenly, to read his name at the bottom of the letter addressed simply to "The Malloy Family," Elise was startled by the unwelcome recollection. She began reading again from the beginning, but his words were obscure, even vague. All she could discern was that a representative from her family must appear at the bank for a meeting because of the "impending circumstances" regarding their house on Mount Vernon Street. There was no clue as to the reason, only an appointed date and time.

Frowning, Elise tossed the letter onto the buffet table in the front parlor and started to walk away. Thinking better of it, she picked it up once more, folded it carefully, and tucked it into the waistband of her skirt.

Reed would be furious if he found out she'd hidden it from him, and truthfully, she hoped he would never find out. He was starting to look for a home of his own, something at the waterfront in a district their mother would never consider proper, but which Reed liked. If he thought his family's home was in peril, he would drop everything to focus on their well-being.

No, she couldn't let him do that. He might jeopardize his career. She would simply meet with the man, herself. The vaguely menacing words might be a misunderstanding, and she could solve the problem with no one in her family becoming the wiser.

Pouring a cup of coffee from the silver urn, she stirred in a spoonful of sugar and added some cream before sitting down alone in the sunshine of the lovely June morning. She picked up the *Boston Post*, considering the front page without really seeing it. She couldn't deny a frisson of anxiety, like something unpleasant tickling her spine, at the prospect of seeing Michael Bradley again.

With a deep breath, she tamped the feeling down. A lot of time had passed, her father was gone, and she had matured. It didn't matter a whit to her what the man thought of her personally.

She'd never spoken with him again since that day at the courthouse. Of course, she'd run into him once or twice socially, or rather, avoided him at all costs if she spotted him at some event she was attending. Not that she'd been looking for him. But he had the sort of demeanor, tall and commanding, that stood out in a room, whether the large marbled foyer of the bank or one of Boston's treasured ballrooms.

In some ways, he reminded her of her brother, both in his height, his presence, and his reputed intelligence. However, there was one thing about this overly confident, handsome—*now why had that ridiculously irrelevant thought occurred to her?*—this banker that was nothing like her brother. Mr. Bradley had displayed arrogance, the essence of self-assuredness.

"Cocky bastard," she declared aloud, finally focusing on the news story in front of her. *The first Kentucky Derby winner at Churchill Downs in Louisville, KY.* "The gallant Aristides, heir to a mighty name, that strides with sweeping gallop toward victory." And the horse wasn't even favored to place.

Suddenly, her mother was there, leaning over her shoulder, having entered on quiet, slippered feet. "Ten thousand people in attendance! Goodness gracious," Evelyn Malloy said. "But I thought you mentioned something about a cock fight."

Elise froze. "No, Mama, a horse race. Come sit with me and have some coffee."

Elise alighted from her practical conveyance, a lovely little Palmer & Doucet two-seater carriage made on the north shore in West Amesbury. It gave her a measure of independence, despite the fact that she was as firmly under her brother's protection in her mother's house as she'd been under her father's before he'd passed.

One step, two steps along Devonshire Street, and she looked up at the daunting, gray granite facade and graceful arches of the Massachusetts National Bank. Although nearly brand new, as most of the street had burned in the great fire just a few years earlier, it somehow managed to look ancient and imposing.

She swallowed, squaring her shoulders and adjusting her hat before she patted her favorite blue velvet purse with its silk cord handle and secure clip closure, assured that the cursedly ominous bank letter was secure inside it.

A bowler-clad doorman whisked open the door for her before she could even touch the handle. He bowed, she nodded, and then she hesitated. Normally, she would head toward a clerk, but today was different.

"I'm here to see, Mr. Bradley," she told the man. "I have an appointment."

"Just so, miss," he said, and gestured to another man, who nodded as the doorman instructed him to "Please show this young lady to Mr. Bradley's office."

Elise followed the man with slicked back hair across the white marble floor, so shiny she could see her reflection as she looked down. She wore one of her favorite pale peach skirts and matching jacket, the color of which so well set off her dark hair, a trait all the Malloy children had inherited from their father's Irish side.

She wasn't trying to look her best or even impress Mr. Bradley. *Of course not!* She merely wanted the confidence that looking shipshape brought to her. Besides, this skirt had a lovely draped bustle and a secondary overskirt in a slightly paler color of peach pulled narrowly around her legs. She felt quite put together.

Distracted by her heeled shoes clicking across the floor, she looked up to find herself in a small waiting area in front of a row of office doors. Here, the man left her with a small bow. Elise didn't have time to take a seat before the tall figure of Michael Bradley appeared in the doorway directly in front of her.

Halting for a moment, his eyes widened before a broad smile spread over his face. His forward motion resumed, and he approached her, taking her hand in his even before she offered it. He held it a moment, looking down at her with the lovely fawnlike green-brown eyes she remembered. All at once, it became difficult to breathe.

"Miss Malloy," he greeted her, his deep voice displaying barely a trace of a Boston accent.

"Mr. Bradley," she said, and that was all she managed.

"I confess I am surprised to see you."

As Elise registered his words, he released her hand.

"Why surprised?" she asked. "You did send a letter to my home. And you couldn't expect my mother to come."

"No, but surely your brother—"

"Is incredibly busy," she finished.

He frowned. "Too busy to protect his family's estate?"

She bristled, not liking the intimation that Reed wasn't looking out for his family's best interests. At the same time, her heart seemed to kick into her throat. What was the extent and seriousness of the problem? It sounded dire.

"He would have come if he'd known about the letter," she said.

"Ah," Michael Bradley's face softened. "I see. You've decided to come in his stead, and without giving him the opportunity."

"Well . . . yes," Elise admitted. "I share an equal interest in my family's well-being, and I like to think my mind is sharp enough to comprehend whatever you have to tell me."

"Oh, I'm sure you're quite sharp enough, Miss Malloy. Won't you come this way?" He gestured for her to precede him into his office with a wave of his arm and the slightest of bows.

"Please, take a seat," he added to the back of her, and she felt his sonorous voice run down her spine like fingertips.

Quickly, she took the closest seat, plushly upholstered in an alternating dark-and-light blue striped brocade.

"Would you care for some tea?" he asked her.

"I prefer coffee," she said, tugging off her gloves. Actually, at that moment, she would prefer a glass of sherry to calm her nerves. Watching him, specifically his large, capable hands as he lifted the tureen from the sideboard, Elise breathed deeply and let her breath out slowly. There was no reason to be nervous.

After pouring the coffee, Michael Bradley slid the white porcelain cup and saucer toward her, looking a little uncertain.

"I usually take it light and sweet," she said.

"My apologies." He frowned, then looked back at the sideboard, obviously searching for the accoutrements. "The clerk who normally offers refreshments is out with some ailment. You're my first customer of the day."

"That's quite all right," she said, reaching for the cup at the same moment that he did, feeling every nerve ending vibrate where his fingertips brushed against hers. Startled, she rattled the saucer and tipped the cup.

His glance shot to hers, and for a moment, they simply stared at each other.

After an embarrassingly long interval, Elise lowered her gaze.

"Drats!" she exclaimed at seeing what she'd done. "I've spilled coffee on your desk."

"My fault," he said.

Yes, it *was* his fault, she thought, for being so darned captivating.

However, all she said was, "No, it was entirely mine. If you could find a serviette, I'll . . ."

However, instead he grabbed a small glass sugar bowl from the sideboard and placed it on the desk next to the spill. Looking around again, he seemed to be expecting a towel to drop from the ceiling.

After a brief hesitation, Elise watched him take a starched white handkerchief out of his pocket and soak up the liquid, then drop the stained cloth next to the tureen.

Unable to keep from looking at him, she managed to over-sweeten her black coffee and make it positively undrinkable.

"There, we've managed to sort that out," he said, as if they'd just discovered the cure for small pox.

"Indeed," she said, relaxing a bit because he seemed so genuine and not nearly as insufferably arrogant as she'd imagined him to be.

And then he ruined it. "So, your family has got itself into a bit of a situation, I'm afraid, but I have no doubt I can set it right."

There was the cockiness she'd always perceived in his self-possessed gaze. If he thought she was going to fall all over him with gratitude, he was sadly mistaken.

"Precisely what *is* the situation? Perhaps my family can muddle through *without* your assistance." She leaned back, sipped the rich, slightly smoky-tasting beverage, and coughed, trying to look nonplussed.

He frowned and cleared his throat. "To be precise, a loan was taken out with this bank using your house as collateral. The note has fallen into default. If you don't pay it in full within a month, then the bank takes your house."

She felt herself pale. The nauseating image of her mother on the front steps of their home with her trunks and furniture on the sidewalk appeared before Elise's eyes.

"Who took out the loan?" she asked.

"Why, your father, of course."

She shook her head. "That's impossible. Father was incredibly successful. He was still booking clients just before he passed away." She remembered Reed offering to help all of them, although some thought her brother was too young to do the quality legal work of their father. He'd proven them all wrong.

"My brother doesn't know about this?" It was a question, although she was sure the answer was no. If Reed had known, he would have discussed it with her at least, even if he'd kept it from their mother.

Michael Bradley shrugged. "That, I don't know. Your mother, of course, has inherited the liabilities of your father, as well as any assets. She must repay the loan or risk foreclosure. Do you know what that means?"

He hadn't asked his question rudely, but rather as if he had a frank desire to explain everything to her. Still, it irked her. She set the coffee cup on his desk with a resounding clack.

"Of course I do." She had no doubt Reed would pay off the loan himself, but probably at some financial hardship.

"May I see the documents, please, Mr. Bradley?"

"Yes, of course," he said, even though she thought he had a slightly condescending expression on his face as if he doubted her ability to understand a legal contract.

Clearly, he had no idea what it was like to grow up in a family of lawyers. Elise watched him open a folder already lying atop his desk, pull out a few sheets of paper, and take the one off the top, which he then held out to her. "This is the summation."

She took it, hoping her hand wasn't visibly trembling, and perused it, but when her eyes came to the amount, she couldn't contain the gasp of dismay.

"Three thousand dollars! But what did my father need such a sum for?"

"That, Miss Malloy, I cannot say. The bank does not ask why, only how much."

*Good God!* She shook her head, considering. How could they pay this off quickly enough to save their home without her father's income? Most certainly, they had that sum sitting in the bank, but it was a sizable amount, and no doubt it would cause them to alter their present lifestyle. And what of Sophie's music education?

Looking up, Elise found Michael Bradley's intense gaze fixed upon her. She swallowed.

"You said you could 'set it right.' What did you mean by that?"

It irritated her to ask him, bothered her even more to be beholden because until that moment, they were on an even footing. Yet he didn't look smug as she had feared he would at her question. Instead, his countenance was one of concern.

"Your family is well-known and has always been in good standing with this bank, since long before I came to work here. History bespeaks volumes in this case. I could take it up with the board of directors and ask them to extend the loan's deadline, create a new schedule of payments, something along the lines of a small monthly payment."

She nodded. *Could it be so simple?*

But there was something puzzling her. "Where have the loan statements been going? To what address? Someone knew about this loan, someone who was ignoring the demands for payment."

She saw it then, a flicker, the merest shadow cross his face. He knew something else that he wasn't telling her.

"There *is* a primary address," he said, "a residence to where the loan payment requests have always gone. And payments were being made until your father's death. Then over the past year, the payments stopped, and the bank simply waited for the loan to go into default."

"Will you give me that address?" Elise asked before she even knew why. For whom had her father taken out a loan, and who would be so careless as to let it go unpaid for so long?

"Will you let me take you to dinner?"

# CHAPTER TWO

His words reached her distracted brain a moment after he spoke them and caused her second gasp of the meeting.

"I beg your pardon?" she said. *Had she heard him correctly?*

"I asked if you will have dinner with me, Miss Malloy. Sometime. Soon." He finished his sentence with his hands clasped on the desk in front of him, his expression earnest, almost one of entreaty.

"I . . . ," she began, but found herself at a loss for words, reduced to clamping her lips closed in case she blurted out something stupid. *Michael Bradley was asking her to dinner!*

He cocked his head at her hesitation. "Will you give me your answer?"

Hadn't they been discussing something vitally important before he had surprised all intelligent thought out of her head?

"Will you give me the address to where the loan statements have been sent?" she asked again.

"Are you saying yes to my invitation?" he persisted.

Is almost seemed as if he were coercing her into having dinner with him. And for some reason, that wasn't bothering her as it should—especially given how he'd previously humiliated her in the courthouse lobby. Truthfully, his strange invitation didn't offend her. In fact, the idea that this very civilized man, in his well-tailored gray suit, would use such primitive tactics to be in her company was, she had to admit, more than a little thrilling.

Nevertheless, she couldn't let him know that. Any self-respecting woman ought to be outraged. Moreover, there was the certain fact that he fully expected her acquiescence, no doubt assuming she still had feelings for him.

Try as she might, however, she could not work herself into high dudgeon over it. Inwardly, she sighed. Being the eldest Malloy child and a proud one at that, it was her duty to take umbrage. Snatching her gloves off her lap, she rose to her feet.

"Are you saying your offer of assistance with this matter is contingent upon my taking an evening repast with you?"

He stood up slowly, the earnest look gone, replaced by the shield of an emotionless mask. Instantly, she knew Michael Bradley displayed that guise to protect himself. She'd seen it on her brother, a reserved man who'd rather grind his molars than ever let anyone see when he felt vulnerable.

"I'm simply pointing out that we have been . . . aware of each other for nearly two years. After spending only a few minutes in your company, I know I would like to become further acquainted with you. We could do that over dinner."

He paused and glanced out his office window before locking gazes with her again. "I am aware a woman of your quality has many suitors, so I suppose I am trying to make my own suit stand out. To such a purpose, I am putting it to you that I would be more likely to plead your case to the board if in turn you allowed me the opportunity to spend time with you."

She pursed her lips. That sounded like blackmail, although dinner with Michael Bradley seemed an easy price to pay.

"Otherwise," he continued, "I suppose you might discard my dinner invitation out-of-hand. But with the added incentive, I assume you will consider it more strongly."

Her mouth had dropped slightly open. Why was this deliciously handsome man—*she could no longer deny her intense attraction to him*—stooping to such tactics? Was there any single female who would *not* accept his offer of dinner? She knew he had stopped seeing the young woman he'd been involved with at the time her father asked after him.

*Was there something wrong with him?*

Involuntarily, her gaze drifted down to the front of his trousers. As soon as she realized what she'd done, she hurriedly lifted it back up to his astounded face.

She felt her cheeks heat up, no doubt richly colored with red. He might think she was considering intimate relations with him to get his assistance. This had become almost farcical, and she had to put a stop to it at once.

"I am afraid it is out of the question." *Why?* she berated herself. Because any woman who would let herself be coerced into spending time with a man was certainly no lady. Their relationship would be soiled from the start. *What relationship?*

"Why is it 'out of the question'?" he asked, keeping his voice reasonable although she could tell he was not pleased by her refusal. "You were interested in making my acquaintance at one time."

*He had not brought that up again, had he?* She felt her former humiliation keenly, as if it were only just happening. He had smiled smugly at her in front of everyone at the courthouse! He had embarrassed her beyond anything!

But what reason could she give for not going out with him? *Think,* she commanded herself. She certainly couldn't tell him her theory about starting a soiled relationship in case he had nothing long-term in mind. Her imagination had run too far ahead, and now she would have to invent an excuse.

"Because I have a beau, and I am close to becoming engaged." *Oh, goodness!* The words had rushed out almost of their own accord. She watched him frown, no doubt in disbelief, and she heard herself add, "Indeed, it might happen at the Crowninshields' party this very weekend."

She watched his nostrils flare ever so slightly at the same time as his eyes narrowed. Then he seemed to dismiss his thoughts with a lift of his shoulder.

"I see. My apologies for overstepping. It was meant actually partly in jest. Of course, you may have the loan's address, and I will do my best for you when I speak with the board next week, regardless."

He crossed his arms.

*Oh!* So, the blackmail was merely a jape. He was toying with her, and now she'd given herself an imaginary suitor. Honestly, her silly spontaneity was far more like something her youngest sister, Rose, would get herself into.

Elise blew at a stray lock of her hair that had found its way out from under her hat and fallen over her forehead. In the silence, his intense gaze seemed to observe the wayward tress lift up and settle back. Then, since he couldn't sit again while she remained standing, he leaned over and pulled a clean sheet of bank stationery from his desk and begin to write. Efficiently, he blotted the ink, folded the paper, and moved around the desk. He held the paper out to her.

She took it, making sure their fingers didn't touch this time. And despite the carefully perfect folds, she immediately opened it. Glancing down, she frowned.

"What about the name of the residence's owner?"

He shook his head. "We only had your father's name. No other."

She nodded.

"Thank you, Mr. Bradley. I appreciate your assistance."

However, if she thought she would escape without further consternation, she was wrong. First, he took her hand in his and held it while the warmth of his touch scorched a trail right through her.

"I hope you did not take offense, Miss Malloy. I went about that invitation all wrong. Had I known you were otherwise involved with someone, I wouldn't have presumed to ask you out at all. It was unknown to me that you had a firm alliance." He appeared annoyed at his lack of knowledge.

*Had he been asking others about her?*

"You did no harm, really," she said and tugged back her hand, which was tingling.

"I'll see you on Saturday evening," he added.

Her heart seemed to stop and then restart. "Whatever do you mean?"

"I'm going to the same party. Crowninshield is my uncle. I'll enjoy meeting your beau," he added.

In truth, she thought he didn't sound as if he would enjoy that at all. For her part, she felt a wave of dread.

"I, as well," she murmured.

"I beg your pardon," he said.

"I mean, I, too, shall enjoy introducing him to you." *Please don't ask his name*, she prayed and was relieved when he didn't. She made it to the door, her brain already in a whirl as to how she would find a pretend suitor in just a few days.

Then a thought occurred to her. "If you would be so kind, please don't mention the loan should you happen across another member of my family. At least, not until I can consider a solution. In any case, perhaps you will have success with the board. Then there will be no need to worry anyone."

He hesitated, but at last, he nodded ever so slightly.

"Good day, Miss Malloy," he said, his gaze never wavering from hers.

"Good day, Mr. Bradley."

Elise drove through the streets without her usual caution. So many problems circled in her head. First, how to find a man who wanted to marry her. Second, how to break off with him so she could instead begin a romantic association with Michael, as she'd come to think of him. Third, find the person who had defaulted on the loan, and fourth, if necessary, pay off the loan.

She was fairly certain her prioritization of the problems was not in the correct order, but she couldn't help that. She would be positively mortified if she couldn't find a man she could introduce as her suitor to the handsome banker during the party.

Her mind scanned her group of friends and quickly discarded each and every one. Then all at once, it hit her: Ethan Nickerson. True, he was nearly old enough to be her father, and yes, he spent as much time in the company of her mother as with her. However, Elise was certain he would immediately play the dutiful suitor if she gave him the slightest encouragement. If that didn't work, she would beg him for the favor. After all, Nickerson was still a fairly attractive man, had all his hair, and walked straight and tall. Some said he was as wealthy as Midas.

For one evening, she could bear having him as her beau, as long as she could break up with him when the night was over. And, of course, the alliance had to look believable to Michael.

That plan more than took care of her first two problems. She glanced again at the address written in Michael's no-nonsense handwriting: *120 Warren Street, Roxbury.*

She knew the area just outside of Boston proper. It was a beautiful avenue with gorgeous homes, and not what she was expecting for some extortionist as she now feared had taken hold of her family. She decided to drive there immediately and see for herself.

Drawing back on the reins, she stopped her carriage across the wide street from a grand home. While the horse pawed the ground, she sat considering who was inside. For whom would her father have taken out a loan, and why?

*What to do, Elise?* she asked herself. Mostly, she wanted to consult with Reed, but something inside of her whispered a warning. If her father hadn't told his son, there must be a good reason.

She could do one of two things: She could go up to the door and knock, thereby immediately discovering who lived there, or she could go back to City Hall and look up the owner.

Chewing upon her lower lip, in another instant, she climbed out of her carriage, hobbled her horse with the reins, straightened her hat, and crossed the street. No time like the present.

Passing through the opening in a low stone wall, she walked along the driveway that wound its way across the well-manicured lawn, and then she was at the impressive front entrance. She knocked.

In a minute, the door swung open, and a smartly dressed maid stood there, neither aloof nor immediately welcoming.

"May I help you, miss?"

"I'm here to see, um . . ." *Who was she there to see?* "I would like to see your employer."

The girl narrowed her eyes. "Is he expecting you, miss?"

"No," Elise admitted. "Is he terribly busy? Perhaps I could see your mistress instead."

At once, the girl shook her head, and her face took on a decidedly unfriendly expression. After all, a maid could get into serious trouble for letting in the wrong person. "There is no Mrs. Amory," the maid said. "I'm afraid you'll have to go now."

Elise had never been turned away from a home before, but that was because she was a Malloy. No doubt she had only to mention her name and . . .

Then it struck her. *Amory!* There was only one Amory who had dealings with her family. No, Reed would not like this at all.

"Please tell Mr. Owen Amory that Miss Malloy is here. I won't take up much of his time. If he is busy, tell him I've just come from the bank. I'm sure he'll see me. Now, I would like to wait indoors. I can feel a bit of a breeze on my neck." And she pushed her way inside past the astonished maid.

"Yes, miss. I'll go tell him directly." Off she scurried. It was not a minute later before the maid returned. "Mr. Amory will see you in the parlor, miss. This way. Sorry to have kept you waiting."

She led Elise through a double-door in the hall into a richly furnished room and gestured for her to sit on the red-velvet settee, which she declined. Giving a shallow curtsey, the maid disappeared through the doorway in the back of the room.

Elise had forced her way in there, but now that she awaited Mr. Amory, her stomach felt as though busy bees were trying to escape. Celia's father was behind this awful loan business, the very same Celia who had tried to trap Reed into marriage while she was *enceinte* with some other man's babe. The same girl who had changed her brother from a jovial, light-hearted youth into a reserved, mistrustful man.

Elise's own father had made Cecelia disappear to the Continent after Owen Amory had threatened Reed's law career. It wasn't known widely outside of the Malloy household, but within her own family, the bad behavior of the Amorys was legendary.

Yes, her brother would be livid if he knew she was in the Amory house.

"Well, well, well," said a male voice.

When Elise turned, it was not the senior Amory she saw, but his son, who had gone to Dane Law School at Harvard a few years before Reed. She searched her memory for his given name but came up blank.

"To what do I owe this unexpected pleasure, Miss Malloy?" No one had ever made the word *pleasure* sound less pleasant.

She didn't answer his question. "You are Owen Amory's son, are you not?"

He flashed a smile that did not reach his eyes. "I am." He gave a little click of his heels as if he'd been in the military although she was fairly certain he had not, and then he offered a slight bow of his head, which did not in any way represent a nod of respect.

Finally, he looked her boldly in the eye. "I am Jonathan Amory, at your service."

She doubted that. He was exuding anything but servitude.

"Thank you for seeing me, Mr. Amory. I expected to meet with your father."

"We did not expect you at all," Jonathon retorted. "Or I assure you, he would have been up and ready, and we would have had a tea tray laid out for such a lovely lady."

Despite the compliment, the expression in his eyes did not soften.

"Won't you have a seat?" he asked.

At that moment, after a light tap on the door, a different maid came in carrying a silver tea service. Elise sighed. The niceties had begun. If only they could speak plainly, but no, they had to sip tea and dance around the subject until one of them gave in.

Taking a seat, she allowed the maid to pour the infernal tea that she despised, and then she took a shortbread biscuit from the tray. After a few moments of imbibing and nibbling had taken place, they both set their saucers and cups back upon the tray.

"I am sorry to come uninvited, Mr. Amory, and it may be that I need to speak to your father in any case, if you are not privy to a certain arrangement between my father and yours."

He barely blinked. "Of course I am aware of the arrangement," he said, his voice cold despite the small smile he tried to bestow.

"Then you must know why I am here."

"I assure you, I do not."

She refrained from sighing again. "There is the matter of the loan coming due," she said.

"That was your father's problem," he said at once, brushing a crumb from his lap.

Elise tightened her jaw at his dismissal. "As you are well aware, my father is deceased."

"Then it is your mother's problem. Why bother us now?" he asked.

"If you are privy to the matter at hand, then you must be aware the bank's payment requests have been coming to this address and not to my home."

He sniffed. "The agreement my father had was with your father. It became null and void in my estimation at your father's demise."

*Cold-hearted bastard!* she thought. "And that agreement was what, precisely?"

He pursed his lips.

"If you won't elaborate, then I must insist on speaking with Mr. Amory, senior."

"He is indisposed."

How convenient. Stonewalling was such an annoying tactic.

"I assume all this has to do with your sister," she surmised.

Jonathon stiffened visibly.

Elise continued, "Obviously this is related to my father stepping in to make sure neither Celia nor your father harassed my brother any further."

Jonathon Amory's jaw clenched. "The agreement was intended to do right by my sister with whom your brother had amorous congress, may I remind you. And she was with child."

"But not my brother's," she pointed out.

"So you say." Crossing his arms, Jonathon leaned back against the settee.

"So my brother said, and he never, ever lies," Elise asserted. "Can you say the same of your sister?"

He flinched as if she'd slapped him.

"Your brother would not have been in the pickle he found himself if he had not laid hands on Celia."

"Agreed," she said. There was no doubt Reed had chosen the wrong young woman with whom to dally. But Celia had had more hands than only Reed's on her, and that was what had got her into trouble. She was carrying someone else's baby when she'd decided Reed was going to pay the price.

"When your father started making threats," Elise continued, trying to keep her tone as businesslike as possible, "my father did what exactly?"

Jonathon sighed as if there was no point in prevaricating any longer. "He offered to pay for her passage to the Continent and for a small flat in Paris."

At least they were finally getting to the meat of the matter, but Elise couldn't help shaking her head. "What about the man whom she eventually confessed was father to her babe?"

Jonathon gave a shudder. "He is out of the picture completely."

Elise decided not to pursue that unsavory business. "But why did my father . . . ?" she trailed off.

"At the time," Jonathon said, "my father would not spend a dime to help Celia. He was too outraged, and rightly so. While he would bully in order to get her a husband, he would only ship her off to Paris with *your* father's money."

Elise nodded. *Her dear father.* Evidently, Oliver Malloy would have done anything to protect his son's career, which would have undoubtedly suffered. Reed's whole reputation would have been sullied if word had got out of his dalliance with Celia Amory. Even with the child not being his, he would have been tainted.

Jonathon uncrossed his legs and leaned forward. "In a moment of weakness, my father agreed to pay the money back over time because, ultimately, Celia was his burden. However, with his position at the bank, he didn't want his name associated with the loan."

Only then did she recall that old Mr. Amory had something to do with finances.

"My brother doesn't know about this arrangement," Elise said, more to herself than to Jonathon Amory.

"I suppose not."

No, because Reed would never have allowed their father to do it if he could have stopped him. Oliver Malloy, having three daughters of his own, had probably felt sorry for the motherless girl with a father who refused to pay to remove her from the country, not even to give her back some scrap of a life.

"Your father was dutifully paying the loan back and then stopped. Why?" Elise pressed.

Jonathon Amory shrugged. "Your father died, and that was the end of it."

That was most certainly not the end of it! "There is still a substantial amount left on the loan. And it was a grave oversight to simply let the payments lapse. Your father defaulted, and the bank wants *our* home."

Mr. Amory sniffed and could not have possibly looked less concerned.

"I guess you shall have to tell your brother, at last, what a steep price there was to his using Celia as his whore."

Elise gasped. "He did no such thing. He loved your sister."

Jonathon shrugged. "As I said, this arrangement was between your father and mine. And my father is no longer willing to pay for Celia's mistakes. She's had no contact with us anyway since she went to France."

"I cannot believe any man of Owen Amory's standing would behave thusly."

Jonathan's mouth tightened. "My father has not been well, and he isn't going to keep sinking money month after month to pay off this debt. That is final."

Elise stood up, unable to remain seated in his company. "Someone should have told my family a year ago, when it was a monthly sum and not a huge single payment that could cripple us."

He rose to his feet. "This conversation is at an end, Miss Malloy. Please don't return. If you do, I'll go straight to your brother."

"Are you washing your hands of your sister?"

He laughed with absolutely no mirth. "You mean will *I* pay off this debt? Absolutely not. I was only two years ahead of your brother at Harvard, and our careers have been quite similar. Our finances are probably equal. I did not enjoy the affair. Why should I pay for it?"

*Why, indeed?* Jonathon had spoken the truth, except that Reed's career had far outshone his. In fact, if anyone was in a better financial situation, it was undoubtedly her brother.

She shook her head. "I hope your father will reconsider. It seems as though he was acting quite honorably up until the time that mine died."

"Honorably or foolishly, that all depends on how you look at it. If your father wanted to finance Celia's emigration, that was his business. However, I do suggest you keep everything quiet, Miss Malloy."

"And why is that? It seems your father's defaulting on a gentleman's agreement could only reflect poorly on your family, not on mine."

"If word gets out that Oliver Malloy took out a loan to pay off my sister, no one will ever believe Reed didn't father Celia's child, will they?"

He gave her a sneer of a smile.

She would not dignify his threat with a response. Without another word, she turned on her heel and left the Amory parlor and their house in short order.

Driving home, she could not entirely fault the son. Why should he pay for the sins of the father or the sister? On the other hand, why should she, her mother, and her sisters pay for Celia either?

Reed had been hurt and duped and then left with nothing but a hardened heart. And she swore on her father's soul that none of this would ever reach her brother's ears.

# CHAPTER THREE

Saturday arrived so quickly, Elise felt as if the world were turning faster than usual. It wasn't the most exciting of parties, not something she usually looked forward to with more than a wearisome agreement to accompany her mother and sisters. However, knowing she would see Michael again made her look forward to the upcoming gathering more than any she'd attended all year, and she was beyond eager for the appointed hour.

Dressing with care in a burgundy gown of rich taffeta, scooped low and very full in the back, she had the maid help to dress her hair in a graceful chignon. Lastly, putting on her favorite dancing slippers, Elise anticipated a gratifying evening.

The trickiest part would be arriving early enough so she could spot Ethan Nickerson and have a private chat with him. Urging her sisters and her mother to arrive promptly at the Crowninshields' home rather than fashionably late was taxing. When all else seemed to fail and they were still dawdling, she told them she might be developing a headache.

"We'd best get there with haste," she said, putting fingers to her temple, "if we are to have any time for socializing at all. Once my headache blooms, we shall have to leave."

Already tense from deceiving her family, Elise thought she might actually have a headache before the evening was over. Moreover, she had to worry about Reed. Although back from Maine, he almost certainly would not attend. He didn't like this sort of social affair, as he was too preyed upon by hopeful young women. Elise fervently prayed he would not have a change of heart. For with certainty, Reed would take one look at her encouraging Mr. Nickerson and demand an explanation.

And if Michael showed up and started talking to Reed, that would be even worse.

Luckily, she spotted her quarry almost immediately. Elise left her sisters and mother still checking their coats and hurried toward Mr. Nickerson.

The distinguished gentleman seemed to watch her approach first with an interested and then with an astonished expression spreading over his craggy face.

"Miss Malloy," he greeted her with a courteous nod. "I hope you are well."

Taking a deep breath, she gave him what she hoped was a winsome smile. It wasn't his fault he didn't make her pulse jump, not the way simply looking at Michael caused her heart to race. Why hadn't she accepted the banker's invitation to dinner? Why did she have to be so proud?

"Mr. Nickerson, I'm glad to run into you. What a happy fluke."

"Not such a happenchance meeting, Miss Malloy." He gave her a curious look. "My secretary said you spoke with him directly to inquire whether I would be in attendance."

*Drat!* She blushed.

"True," she said. "I admit," only because she'd been caught, "that I hoped to see you here. It has been too long since you were in our home and in my company."

He smiled cautiously. He was no fool, and she felt a pang of guilt.

Elise was about to place her hand on his arm and flutter her dark eyelashes as she had seen their incorrigible Rose do, when Nickerson looked past her, over her right shoulder. Expecting to see her mother and sisters, Elise turned to find Jonathon Amory standing nearby as if waiting to speak with her.

She frowned. He was interrupting her desperate attempt to get a suitor, and the last thing she wanted to do was discuss the bank loan while her family was close at hand. She firmly gave him her back once more.

"Miss Malloy," came his voice, proving the man to be even nearer than he'd been a moment before. "May I have the courtesy of a word with you?"

She took a deep breath and glanced at him again. He didn't appear as if he was leaving any time soon. She cast a rueful look at Nickerson.

"Excuse me. I'll be back in due course." She curtsied low, gave him another dazzling smile, and followed Mr. Amory.

They walked toward a deserted section of the room, next to a drafty window, a potted plant, and fortunately, a table of glasses brimming with citrus rum punch.

Taking a glass, Elise sipped delicately. *Delicious.* She took another taste. He watched her in silence. She didn't have time for this. She had a suitor to conjure.

"Yes, Mr. Amory. What more can you wish to say? After our last meeting, I didn't expect to speak with you again, except perhaps in court."

He smiled tightly, yet he seemed somehow different, less hostile than when she'd bearded him in his home earlier in the week.

"I've been considering your visit."

She allowed a flurry of hope to dance through her brain. Perhaps he would pay off the bank loan, and that problem, at least, would be settled.

"I may have been somewhat terse with you," he said, his tone far more agreeable than it had previously been.

In her estimation, he had rushed straight past 'terse' and stopped at 'rude.' She sipped again and found it quelled her unease.

Then Jonathon Amory added, "I hope my family has not caused your widowed mother any discomfit."

Well, if Elise had actually told her mother, then—

"I think I have come up with a solution that will bring us both satisfaction," he offered.

"Very well, Mr. Amory. I'm listening."

She *was* listening and drinking the scrumptious punch, and only half-noticed that his gaze swept her from head to toe.

"I think we should be married," he said at last.

Somehow, Elise found herself spraying the front of the man's impeccably tailored suit coat with the punch she'd been about to swallow. Coughing and choking at the same time, she felt tears roll down her cheeks as she tried to breathe.

While she regained her composure, her would-be fiancé waited, gingerly wiping at his jacket with a handkerchief although failing to offer her one.

"I beg your pardon," Elise said when she had caught her breath and wiped her cheeks with her fingertips.

"It is all right," he said. "I'm sure my man servant can clean it. And tonight, no one will notice after it dries."

"No, Mr. Amory. I mean, I beg your pardon, did you just ask me to marry you?"

"Yes, I did."

"Whatever for?" That sounded impolite, but his question, out of the blue, was beyond the pale.

"If you were my wife," he said in a hushed tone, "I would pay the balance owed to the bank. I certainly wouldn't let my wife's mother lose her home."

"And why would you want to do this?"

He shrugged. "At my age, I ought to have a wife, although I will admit to having been extremely unmotivated to acquire one until now. Yet you're available, reasonably attractive," he added, scanning her once more, "and from a good family.

Except for your brother's youthful indiscretion with my sister. And you seem to have a sound mind."

She nodded at his words, even his odd way of paying her a compliment, until he mentioned her brother. Despite him being right even about Reed's youthful indiscretion, she frowned.

"Our families are known to each other," Mr. Amory added.

That was an understatement. She could only imagine Reed's reaction if she were to announce who her new father-in-law would be, not to mention having Celia as a sister-in-law.

"What would your father say to such an arrangement?" she asked.

"He'd be happy to see his only son married at last and, of course, produce an actual heir, not some French bastard."

She shivered. Maybe the idea had merit. But produce an heir with Jonathon Amory? Have amorous congress with him? Goodness! She took his measure, looking at him again with new eyes. She had not a sliver of interest even though he was neither ugly, nor dull-witted. He was, in fact, attractive if one appreciated boyish good looks. But he was not Michael Bradley.

As if she'd conjured him with her thoughts, she noticed the dashing banker had arrived and was making the rounds of the room. She went to take another sip of her punch only to find her glass was empty, so she set it down and picked up another one.

With bad luck, Michael Bradley halted his progress to speak with Mr. Nickerson, and to her horror, they were looking toward her and Jonathon. There was only one thing Elise could do, knowing the duration of the deception would be temporary, perhaps a single day, two at the most.

"Fine, I accept." She took a swig of her punch and stuck out her free hand for him to shake on the deal as she'd seen her brother do.

Jonathon stared at her hand then clasped it. Just at that moment, Michael approached.

"Mr. Bradley," she said, turning to him and feeling more delighted than she ought to. She had no hand to offer him, so she nodded slightly and sipped her drink. The room was becoming so warm despite it not yet being crowded. Then she spied her mother talking to Mr. Nickerson and glancing at her. *Why had the old coot become the center of attention?*

Then it dawned on her she would have to tell her mother the same lie she was going to tell Michael. Feeling the heat rise to her cheeks, she knew she must be exceedingly flushed. She tugged her hand free from Jonathon's grasp.

"It's a pleasure to see you again, Miss Malloy," Michael said in his sonorous voice that made her think of polished oak.

"It's wonderful to see you," she agreed, hearing her own gushing town and unable to help but give him a broad smile. He looked adorably fetching in his dark suit. She thought he'd stepped even closer, but realized she had swayed toward him.

His eyes widened at her enthusiasm. Sighing, she happily stared at him until Jonathon coughed.

Elise glanced at him. "This is Mr. Bradley of the Massachusetts National Bank." She turned back to Michael, momentarily forgetting to introduce Jonathon.

In any case, Michael didn't seem to care who the man was. Sparing him not more than a cursory glance, he held out his hand to her. "Will you dance with me, Miss Malloy?"

Nodding, she took his outstretched hand, remembering at the last second to hand Jonathon her glass. Michael pulled her along behind him to where partners were lining up for the first dance.

She'd been to her fair share of dances, dinner parties, and soirees, and had even seen Michael at one or two, but she'd never been this close to him before, nor ever had him for a partner. She curtsied, and he bowed as the music began.

As she expected, he was an excellent dancer, and Elise was extremely grateful her mother had schooled all four of her children in the art of dancing. She could glide effortlessly and still carry on a conversation, knowing her feet were doing what they were supposed to, although the punch had slightly slowed her steps.

"You went to the address I gave you," Michael said.

*How did he know?* "Yes, I did."

"Did you find a satisfactory resolution?" he asked.

She thought about the engagement into which she'd just absurdly entered. "Um, so it would seem."

He nodded as each man took his partner into his arms for a clockwise spin around the polished wooden floor. Michael followed suit and twirled her.

Elise caught her breath, held close by him, his strong arms around her, and the world shrunk to only the two of them. He smelled fresh and masculine, vetiver and citrus, and she longed to press her nose against his chest and breathe deeply.

*Good God!* She, herself, probably smelled like rum!

Looking up into his eyes, just as at the bank, she felt caught like a rabbit in a snare, unable to move, unable to look away. And it didn't bother her in the least, except for the pounding of her heart, which she was positive he could hear and feel.

"What happened to your beau?" he asked, his voice low and gentle, but with a hint of teasing.

*Beau? What beau?* Oh! She felt her cheeks heat again. She wanted to tell Michael then and there how very rash she'd been to create an imaginary suitor and how delighted she would be to go to dinner with him, with a suitable chaperone. Opening her mouth to do exactly that, she felt him stiffen.

Suddenly, he was holding her slightly away from him, and she nearly protested out loud, wanting to crush herself against his warmth and feel his arms encircle her once more. However, before she could embarrass herself, another hand tapped his shoulder.

Michael glanced to its owner, and Elise's gaze followed.

Jonathon Amory stood beside them, and before she could say anything to stop him, he tilted his head and asked, "May I have this next dance with my fiancée?"

Elise watched Michael's nostrils flare, his jaw clench, and his eyes widen slightly as his gaze left Jonathon's face and locked onto hers.

She swallowed and offered a smile that probably looked as sickly as she felt. Then his lovely hazel eyes narrowed, and he nodded ever so slightly, releasing her as if she were a hot branding iron, all friendliness vanished.

"Certainly," Michael said, his tone clipped. "I offer my congratulations. I was unaware. However, I take it this is quite a recent development."

"Why, why yes. Very recent," she heard herself stammer.

Luckily, a waiter went by, and even though they were in the middle of the dancers, she caught the man and took another glass of punch off his tray. Her tongue felt surprisingly thick, and she was parched.

In two long sips, it was gone. Puzzled, she eyed the empty glass. It must not have been full to begin with.

Looking from one man to the other—Michael simmering with some unnerving emotion, his tawny gaze drilling into hers, and Jonathon disinterested, even bored—she thought they both were swaying in time to the music. How odd.

"You, gentlemen, are supposed to shake hands," she said, feeling the floor move slightly now as well.

Hiccupping, Elise raised her hand belatedly to cover her mouth. She didn't want to dance anymore. No, not at all. More than anything, she wanted to sit down. Even better, she wanted to stretch out flat on the polished walnut and maple striped surface and close her eyes.

Michael looked to Jonathon, with an ironic upturn of his eyebrow. "I wish you good luck with her, sir."

However, just as he would have turned away, she took a step toward him and reached out her hand, thinking to grasp onto his sturdy looking lapel and perhaps anchor herself. Instead, she got a fistful of his cravat and started to slid down his front. She knew she was going to collapse at his feet, and she couldn't do a blasted thing to stop herself. Her legs had turned to quince jelly.

As she began her descent, his arms came around her to hold her up. In the next moment, he swept his arms under her knees to lift her completely off the floor. Snaking her arms around his neck, she held on.

A murmur went through the crowd at the spectacle she was making. She didn't give a fig.

Heavenly, that's what it was to be in Michael's arms. She sent a lopsided smile up at him, but he merely scowled down at her in return.

Just then, Elise heard her mother exclaim, and all at once, both her sisters and Evelyn Malloy were around her. In the next instant, she reluctantly released her grip as Michael transfer her to another's hold, and Elise looked up into Jonathon's bewildered face. He seemed none too pleased to be holding a swooning woman in the middle of the party.

Turning on his heel, Michael walked away, and Elise craned her head to watch him.

"Thank you," she heard her mother call after him. He lifted a hand in a silent gesture but didn't turn around.

Immediately, her sisters began asking questions, and Sophie reached out to feel her forehead.

"I'm fine, just a liddl warm," Elise said. *Was she slurring her words?*

"You look positively green," her mother said.

"I think I needa chair," Elise managed, desperate to no longer be the center of attention. "I wanna go home," she added.

Rose clapped her hands once, her face delighted. "You're soused."

*Blast!* Her youngest sister shouldn't even be there, but her mother always insisted on bringing all her daughters.

"*Sh*," Sophie quieted her.

"Oh, dear," her mother said, making a clucking sound with her tongue. "That's what comes of not eating before a party."

Evelyn looked to the long-suffering man who had not yet been introduced to her. "My daughter said she wasn't feeling well before we arrived."

"Indeed," was all Jonathon said. "Can you stand now, Miss Malloy?"

"I believe so," she said, although her stomach did a nasty twist when he set her upon her feet.

"Let's get her home," Sophie said, putting an arm around her. Rose took up the other side, and they left with her mother clearing the path in front of them like the prow of a ship.

Elise found herself whisked away from the Crowninshields' home, grateful she hadn't had to explain to her family who Jonathon was. Having him announce himself to Michael had been more than enough of a shock for one evening.

Michael strode out of the party and his uncle's house, sucking in the night air in great heaving breaths. Damn, but he wanted nothing more than to turn around, retrieve Elise Malloy from her so-called fiancé—*what a load of bunkum that was!*—and carry her away.

*Carry her where?* Anywhere they could be alone, anywhere he could hold her in his arms again. He climbed into his phaeton, flicked the reins, and sped off.

Ever since the first time he'd laid eyes on her, he had wanted her for his own. And finally, he'd danced with her, feeling her warmth, experiencing her spirit, and losing himself in her impossibly blue eyes.

A moment later, she was collapsing against him like an unsteady newborn colt. Every instinct in him had screamed to protect her, hold onto her, and yet he'd been compelled to hand her over to Jonathon Amory.

Why would she pretend Amory was the suitor she'd spoken of? She would have known who lived at the Roxbury address he'd given her if it were true. And why would Amory suddenly pretend to be her fiancé? It was maddeningly absurd.

He drove home too fast, charged up his front steps, slammed into his townhouse on Beacon Street, heading directly for his box of expensive cigars. Cut and lit, the cigar provided a measure of comfort as he sat in front of his unlit fireplace and brooded.

Plain as day, Elise had lied to him in his office about having a beau, which he soundly deserved for the foolish way in which he had asked her to dinner. When she'd shown up at the bank rather than her brother, he'd been surprised and delighted to see her again after nearly two years. He'd hoped she'd come because she'd wanted to see him, and he half thought she would be amused at his little jest. He'd been wrong.

He had also expected her to have forgiven him by the time of his uncle's dance and, perhaps, have changed her mind about having dinner with him, for he'd be certain she had no beau. Again, he had been wrong.

Instead, she had taken up with Amory of all people, the very man who was threatening her family's home by reneging on payments. Apparently, her little lie to avoid accepting his invitation had turned into a larger obfuscation. It seemed Elise would do anything rather than have dinner with him.

Or perhaps she would do anything rather than pay off the bank loan, even marry a stranger.

Michael took a long pull from his cigar. For the sake of her lovely eyes, he would take her case to the bank's board and because of her bewitching smile, he would make sure they gave the Malloys an extension based on the hardship of Mr. Malloy's death.

Or he would pay the damn loan back himself.

Most of all, he wanted her to look him in the eye and confess that Amory meant absolutely nothing to her.

# CHAPTER FOUR

Elise awakened in the wee hours of the morning when the bright moon was still high, one end of a downy feather from her pillow poking her in her cheek. The memories of the previous evening rushed back, and she groaned.

She was indeed engaged but to Mr. Amory, not Mr. Nickerson, and not a pretend engagement, either, for the inane purpose of showing Michael she wasn't to be trifled with. Instead, Jonathon Amory had offered to pay the loan in return for her hand in marriage.

Still, if Michael hadn't been approaching so swiftly and if she hadn't taken such a liking to that blasted rum punch, she was certain she wouldn't be engaged that very morning.

Lying awake a long time, Elise tried to sort out her thoughts despite her throbbing head. She had grabbed at the offer from Jonathon with the idea of saving face in front of Michael, and now she had a viable solution to her problem of the unwieldy bank loan. She could marry the man in order to protect her family from financial loss, and at the same time, she could avoid potential scandal for her beloved brother.

Elise turned on her side to avoid the bright moonlight, which managed to slip through a slit in her drapes and throw its glaring beam across her face. Her reason for marrying Mr. Amory was admirable, to be sure, but she couldn't really consider doing so. At least, she didn't think she could. This wasn't the Middle Ages, for goodness' sake!

Then there was Michael. He had given her a particularly disapproving look, although he couldn't possibly know that Amory wasn't really her long-time suitor. Nevertheless, his dismissing, judgmental glance had stung all the same.

Elise had a notion there was little likelihood of his asking her out again, even after she broke off her spontaneous engagement. She'd behaved terribly, drinking too much due to nerves and practically falling at Michael's feet. The thought of it made her stomach churn even then.

Still, she couldn't deny dancing with him and being held by him, however briefly, had nearly made the whole fiasco worth it.

When she finally fell back to sleep, the moonlight had been replaced by the first pinkish rays of dawn. Elise slumbered on until Rose came bounding unbidden into her room at mid-morning, chattering like a magpie.

"Ha, sis, you were exceedingly funny last night," she said, sitting down on the side of the bed.

Elise yawned widely and stretched.

"Was I?" *Good Lord!* What would she tell her mother? And did she have to mention the engagement? Of course not! She had to get to Jonathon Amory first and make sure he said nothing to anyone.

"It seemed you had two gentlemen interested in you last night," Rose continued. "And I didn't recognize either one of them."

*Two gentlemen last night.* And one had asked her to marry him. Some might say it was past time for her to be a wife. As the eldest daughter, her unmarried state was probably holding Sophie back from getting engaged, although Rose was still too young to be thinking about it.

Certainly, over the past few years, Elise had been the recipient of men professing some level of admiration. However, until she'd seen Michael Bradley that day at the bank with her father, she'd never felt the strange and wondrous sensation of truly wanting to know another person and to know him deeply. Nor had she felt it since, not with any of her would-be suitors.

After seeing Michael again, the desire was even stronger to learn his likes and dislikes, to find out what brought him joy, to know how his body would feel under her fingers . . .

"Elise, are you listening?"

"No, I'm not," she confessed. "Go make sure there is fresh coffee, and I'll be downstairs in a few minutes. Hurry up, be a good girl, and leave me in peace to dress."

Rose grinned, probably figuring Elise still had a pounding head, which she did, but her sister skedaddled out of the room with her never-ending energy.

Elise sighed. She was not a young girl anymore. It was high time she considered seriously this whole idea of marriage. But Jonathon Amory? Was he really the best option? Maybe he was her *only* option. She tried to imagine her next home being the Amorys' mansion on Warren Street? That thought brought her no happiness at all, except for offering her the opportunity to help out her family.

The day passed without any further drama, and Elise kept her head down and her thoughts to herself. She knew she should contact her "fiancé," but she wanted to do nothing more than . . . well, nothing at all. Ever since she'd opened that damned bank letter, she'd been bouncing from one unfamiliar situation to another.

When Reed arrived home for supper, Elise looked at her earnest, sincere brother, and her heart melted. She knew she would do nearly anything to spare him a moment of pain, perhaps even marry a man for whom she had no love.

"You've been working very hard," she said to him as they sat beside each other at the dining room table. She couldn't help noticing he'd brought a stack of papers with him to dinner and had his briefcase under his chair.

Only a year and a half apart, they were closer than any of the other siblings, and Elise had always felt him also to be her very good friend. It was doubly difficult not to consult with him on the strange state of affairs in which she currently found herself.

He clasped her hand where it rested on the table, but instead of a weary expression, his face lit up.

"I'm at a turning point in the case. It's incredible what comes out in court when people are under pressure. Just today—"

Evelyn Malloy interrupted her only son. "I told your father years ago, and I will remind you, Reed Perry Malloy, no legal talk while we eat. It's unsettling to your dining companions and bad for the digestion."

Reed grinned. "Yes, Mother, although I do recall our father breaking that rule every so often."

Sophie, their musical middle sister, smiled, too. "At nearly every meal time."

Evelyn smiled. "True. All right, dear boy, tell us if you're winning or losing, and then let it go. You should not be thinking about law cases every hour of your day. Balance is key."

"Agreed," Reed said, "and I'm winning."

They gave him a small round of applause and watched him dig into his food with gusto.

"Excellent," said their mother. "So, in the name of balance, when will you marry and give me a grandchild?"

Elise watched her brother freeze with the fork on its way to his mouth. Then he resumed and stuffed it in, waving his hand at Evelyn to indicate he couldn't speak due to his full mouth.

That very moment would be an agreeable time to take the burden off her brother. Better than anyone, she knew how unhappy he was with being considered one of Boston's most eligible bachelors. At every turn, he was pounced upon by marriageable young women and, in many circumstances, by their mothers who were intent on pleading their daughters' virtues.

Elise could simply announce her engagement and Evelyn would focus her attention solely on her eldest daughter. However, she could not get the words out.

The next day, she intended to visit Jonathon.

This time, she was greeted more warmly by the maid and by Jonathon, too, although his father still did not put in an appearance.

"Does your father not wish to speak with me about this?" Elise asked, curious at his absence while they drank milky tea. She could not imagine her own father or her mother not being all over the prospective spouse.

"He will be at the wedding, I assure you, and he gives us his blessing," Jonathon said, seemingly unperturbed.

*The wedding!* The very words filled her with dread—obviously not the correct emotion for a prospective bride.

"My brother will want to speak with him and with you prior to the ceremony, of course," she said, hardly able to believe she was still considering this madness.

"Hm, I'm not sure about that," Jonathon returned. "Do you think your brother will be violent?"

Elise tried not to show her shock.

"Most assuredly not. However, if this marriage were to happen, I don't want a word about the loan said to him. Any discussion will be strictly about our mutual fondness, the fact that you don't want any dowry, and how you intend to make me happy. Otherwise, he will put a stop to it, I am certain."

"I see."

What exactly did he see? Elise couldn't fathom from his veiled gaze. Then he shrugged and smiled slightly.

"And thus, we are in agreement," he stated, looking away to refill his cup before she could respond.

All at once, she knew she couldn't go through with it. There had to be another way. Did she own something of value she could sell for the lump sum, so no one need ever know about the cursed loan? She could not possibly go into any sort of employment and make the money in time for the bank to stay the foreclosure, nor could she do so without her family finding out. Yet there must be some solution she was overlooking.

If only she could talk to Reed. If she owned the exquisite concert piano in her mother's conservatory, she could sell it, but it belonged to Sophie, given to her by their father.

*What else?* Then she remembered the book.

*Sweetcake, the answers to most of your questions will be found in a book, but the questions, those come from living life.*

And what book had her father waggled at her the day he'd uttered those words, barely two months before he died? It was a book that had been keeping him occupied, one that he'd been carrying around and seemingly reading during every spare moment, a book that had been on his bedside table at the very end.

She tried to remember what it was—a volume of Wordsworth, perhaps.

*Where was that book?* She longed to read it and see if the answers were really inside.

It had to be back in his study, which Reed now used as his own. Occasionally, Elise sat alone in there to speak to her father, even though he had gone where he could no longer offer her his wise counsel. Her mother never entered the room as she said it was too painful. Evelyn could still smell her husband's aftershave. That was what Elise liked about the study, the feeling that he might still be there if she only closed her eyes and listened.

"Please excuse me," she said, jumping up and heading for the door before Jonathon even had time to put down his cup. "I'm sure we will speak again soon."

She fled before he could question her urgent departure.

Less than an hour later, Elise pushed the door open to what had always been Oliver Malloy's sanctuary. The large desk was littered with Reed's papers and law books resting open on some relevant page. It could all as easily have been her father's things. He had died too young although he'd lived a full life, had his beloved wife by his side for over thirty years, and had seen nearly all four of his children into adulthood.

A headache, a fever, and a week later, he was gone. But everything here looked the same.

Taking a seat in his worn leather chair, Elise rested her hands on the armrests and closed her eyes. Leaning her head back, she sniffed the air for her father's aftershave. Nothing . . . except the faint whiff of her brother's favored sandalwood scent.

Opening her eyes, she scanned the desk. Nothing private of Reed's, of course. He would never leave anything in the open. Not a love letter or such. She shook her head. *Why was her head so full of love lately?* And of course, Michael's visage immediately popped into her addled brain.

Absently, she opened the shallow middle drawer and saw it contained only writing implements—metal nibs, extra ink, and blotting papers. In the top drawer on the right, she found a leather-clad notebook.

Glancing inside, she saw her father's familiar scrawl. The first page stated, "A Comprehensive List of My Book Collection."

The list was organized, alphabetized, neat, and precise. He had sold some books, in which case, the title was underlined, not crossed out, and in the far column was the amount he had received. Sometimes quite a generous figure, she noted.

She scanned down to those books that her family still owned. And then it jumped out at her on the third page, a note in the margin: *Caxton for J.P. Morgan.*

Bells went off in her head like Sunday morning on Beacon Hill. Next to the note, it said "$4000."

*Good God!* She'd had the necessary money all the time, and then some.

Behind her in a floor-to-ceiling bookcase were her father's books, except for the William Caxton first edition. It was in her own bedroom, as it had been since before her father's death. He'd told her to look over this valuable piece of history before he sold it.

She smiled to herself and headed for her room.

A few days later, Elise strode into the bank, feeling as though she'd regained a firm foothold where previously, everything had been topsy-turvy. Michael Bradley was expecting her, purportedly to fill her in on how he had fared at the board meeting. She actually had little interest in that because she intended to pay off the loan in full.

Her only reason for going once more to the bank was how desperately she wanted to see him again, despite knowing it was unwise. Her behavior had been beyond the pale, and he considered her an engaged woman. Nevertheless, when he'd sent her a private missive to come in, she'd eagerly grasped at the excuse.

Sitting outside his office, however, she felt the butterflies take flight in her stomach. How would he treat her after her tipsy display? Suddenly, she wondered if she should have come at all.

The door opened while she was arguing with herself, almost ready to flee. Immediately, their eyes locked, and she couldn't have left if she'd wanted to. And she no longer wanted to. All she could think about was being in his arms.

"Miss Malloy, it's . . . good to see you again."

Had he hesitated? Perhaps he hadn't really *wanted* to see her again but had felt it his duty to complete their business. What could she say that wouldn't sound too eager, too ridiculous coming from an engaged woman as he believed her to be?

She supposed she still was but not for long. With the precious Caxton in her possession, she'd already gone to see the trusted book dealer her father always used. He'd astounded her with the price that Mr. Morgan was willing to pay.

Nonetheless, until the transaction was complete and the money was in her hands, she would not visit Jonathon Amory and call off the wedding. In her heart, however, the farce of an engagement was all but over, and she was relieved not to have had to tell her family anything about it or about the loan.

But Michael knew.

He invited her in with a small bow.

"Take a seat. Coffee, Miss Malloy? Our refreshment clerk is back." He offered her a smile.

"Thank you, no." She wished she could tell him to stop addressing her so formally. After all, she'd been held by him. However, that was impossible at this juncture. Looking down, she sighed.

"Everything all right?" he asked. "You're feeling better, I trust."

Her eyes darted from her lap to his face. Was he mocking her?

"Yes, I'm quite well. I suppose I owe you not only my gratitude but also an apology. I'm not in the habit of imbibing such a quantity. I hadn't partaken of any luncheon, and then," she shrugged, "those little glasses of punch were—"

"Were not so little," he offered.

She noticed humor dancing in his hazel-colored eyes.

"Precisely." She relaxed, given his easy manner. "But the concoction was tasty."

"I'll take note you have a liking for rum and citrus."

*Would he really?* she wondered.

"And coffee," he added.

She recalled that Jonathon persisted in offering her tea despite her having told him she did not care for it.

Michael leaned forward, and his eyes seemed to draw her in. "I thought you were going to apologize for something else."

She opened her mouth, then closed it. Finally, knowing she wore a puzzled look, she asked, "For what precisely?"

"Never mind. Perhaps later." He leaned back in his chair. "For now, let me tell you some good tidings."

She let go her confusion over his remark, and said, "Yes, please do."

"The board was extremely favorable to extending the payment schedule and removing any immediate threat to your home."

She breathed easier even though she would have the entire amount in a day or so.

"That's excellent news. Thank you, Michael. I mean . . . oh dear." She felt her cheeks warm and knew she was blushing profusely. In her head, she'd become so used to thinking of him by his first name, it had slipped out. How outrageous!

"I mean, Mr. Bradley," she amended softly, wishing she could disappear under the carpet.

He paused, whether at her using his Christian name or at her obvious distress, she didn't know, but he nodded his head as if nothing had happened.

She noticed he didn't come forth and say, "Please, call me Michael." She would have reciprocated immediately. How she would love to hear her own name on his lips!

"And we can start sending the statements to your house," he was saying with those very same lips when she began listening again.

"No!" she nearly shouted.

Clearing her throat, she clasped her hands in her lap. "I mean. That won't be necessary," she added hastily.

He pursed his lips. "Then I take it you would rather we continue to send them to your fiancé's residence?"

She gasped at his tone.

"You look distressed, Miss Malloy."

"No, I'm fine. I just—"

"You didn't think I knew that Jonathon Amory resided at the address I gave you."

How stupid of her! Of course, he would know, even though he'd said the bank didn't have the name.

"Imagine how very odd I found it that your beau, who so quickly became your fiancé, also belonged to the family for whom the loan had been taken out. And yet you didn't know they were one and the same, didn't even know your own suitor's address. What am I to make of that?"

He was definitely mocking her now. He'd steepled his fingers in front of him on the desk, just the way Reed did when he was pondering the minutiae of a particularly difficult case he was working on.

She swallowed. Michael had caught her out in a bald-faced lie. In fact, she realized that was what he'd expected her to apologize for.

Blowing the stray hair off her forehead, Elise sucked in her lower lip. She couldn't think of anything to say that would make this better. And she longed to know the right words to have Michael look at her again as he'd done when they were dancing?

"You should not try to blackmail women into dining with you," she muttered.

That wasn't what she'd meant to say, and certainly not in that cantankerous tone.

His eyebrows shot up before his mouth formed a grim line of disapproval.

"Are you implying because I asked you to dine with me, I gave you cause to lie, to become *engaged* to Amory, and to drink yourself into a stupor?"

"Oh!" She jumped to her feet. He had gone too far.

He stood, too, but he didn't look apologetic. He looked as if he was merely getting started.

"And yet none of those indiscretions seem even remotely as damning as the fact that you would marry yourself off to a man you don't even know for the paltry sum of $3,000."

Elise felt her cheeks growing hot again, but she had no outlet for her anger. She had done everything of which he'd accused her, and it sounded much worse when he said it to her face. The only person with whom she could be angry was herself. Still, a woman had her pride.

"Everything I did—well, except for lying to you about a beau after your ineptly insulting dinner invitation, may I add," she paused for emphasis, "everything of which you accuse me I did for my family. And I would do it all again, too."

No need to explain to him she hadn't really become engaged to Mr. Amory for the money, nor how she'd meant to use Mr. Nickerson as a suitor. Somehow, that didn't make her sound as if she had an ounce more integrity or sense. She could tell him of the fear she'd felt at possibly losing their home or the absolutely unacceptable risk of Reed's name being brought up in relation to Celia Amory once again. However, that seemed manipulative, as if she were attempting to prompt his sympathy.

Michael could simply think the worst of her, and she could not care less.

This meeting was over. Turning, she headed for the door.

# CHAPTER FIVE

Michael Bradley moved quickly for a banker, and somehow rounded his desk and had his hand beside her head, holding the door firmly closed with the flat of his palm.

Ineffectually, she jiggled the door knob. When she turned, she was practically engulfed by him.

"You began this whole travesty because you didn't want to dine with me?" he asked.

"No," she ground out, looking down at the floor. If she looked up, he'd see in her eyes how much she fancied him.

"Do you like Jonathon Amory? Do you even know him?"

"That's none of your business," she pointed out.

"I am making it my business. Do you care for him?"

He seemed to move closer, his body leaning in, but instead of feeling smothered, Elise wanted to press against him. She couldn't be this close to him and lie again.

"No."

"Do you, in fact, have a beau?" he demanded.

His voice had grown huskier, making her shiver. She squirmed, wanting to flee and at the same time, not wanting to move an inch away from this man. If only he would stop interrogating her.

"No," she confessed.

"Why?"

His voice definitely seemed lower, and it was doing peculiar things, tingly things, to her insides.

"I hadn't met the right man." *Until now.* "I've had offers," she added, trying to salvage some shred of dignity.

"I know you have."

*How did he know?* she wondered.

"I know you were associated with Randall Dexter," he added, "and I'm sorry for your loss."

She started at her friend's name. If he hadn't died, perhaps they would have been married already. But in honesty, she'd felt more sisterly toward him than whatever these stirring feelings were that Michael evoked—causing exciting, yet slightly overwhelming emotions.

"Mr. Bradley, let me go."

"Why won't you look at me?" he asked.

Slowly, she raised her gaze to his, and she would swear a lightning bolt sizzled through her. Seeing a similar response in his expression, Elise even felt it between her hips, making her tingle deliciously. Then he lowered his head, keeping his eyes on hers.

He was going to kiss her. They were alone in his office, and he was going to kiss her. Had she ever been more improper in her life? Had she ever cared less for propriety?

At the last moment, she closed her eyes, and then his lips touched hers. She nearly moaned. Gentle at first and then the slightest pressure, his kiss became firmer.

How could this simple touch create the sizzling sensations throughout her body? But it did. His hands were suddenly at her waist, drawing her close.

She wanted to touch him, too, to feel his hair, to lace her fingers behind his neck and anchor him, but she couldn't. It would be unseemly. In another instant, she was doing precisely that, not caring that her reticule, dangling from her wrist, had smacked them both on the side of their faces as she slipped her hands up and over his shoulders.

Apparently, that was a signal for him to deepen the delightful assault on her senses. His mouth slanted and somehow fit against hers even more perfectly. A small movement he made with his lips and the tip of his tongue caused her to part her own lips. She felt gloriously decadent.

At the same time, he pulled her to fit against the length of his body, while pressing her back to the door. Elise felt the hardness of the wood behind her and the identical hardness of Michael in front of her.

How wondrous! And her body answered. Her heartbeat hammered through her, throbbing in the base of her throat with an echoing sensation between her legs.

Hearing herself moan, Elise felt his body tense in response. While a part of her thought she would be happy to stay right there in his arms, kissing him until the day she died, another part of her knew a longing for something more.

Her instincts told her to nibble at his lips and to sweep her tongue against his, and she did. She heard his answering sound, like a groan or a growl, and it sent a shiver racing through her.

How many long, glorious minutes they kissed, she couldn't say. A hundred or ten. At last, he lifted his head.

Whereas she had been breathing through her nose, she now took in a few gulps of air and saw he did the same.

"Why are you pursuing me?" she asked when she was able to speak.

"I have never forgotten how sweetly your father enquired as to my availability, and how thoughtlessly I ruined any chance with you at the time by being overly forward at the courthouse."

She blushed, thinking of that pivotal encounter.

"I came across as boorish," he continued, raking his eyes over her flushed face, "but I was simply so delighted to see you unexpectedly that day and to know you had an interest in me."

She nodded, unable to deny what she felt then and now.

He smiled and tucked a lock of her hair behind her ear. "Currently, I am entirely unattached, and I must tell you at the risk of humiliating myself, you are the sole reason."

"I am?" Her words came out as a squeak.

"I confess I was flattered by your father's enquiry, but much more than that. I was deeply attracted to you. I couldn't get you out of my mind, Miss Malloy. I say that in all honesty to make up in some small way for how I blundered and caused you such embarrassment. It was entirely unintended."

At his heartfelt confession, Elise thought she might float away, like a butterfly caught in a stiff breeze. She'd had no idea he had even noticed her that first time she'd gone to the bank. Certainly, when she'd asked her father to find out if he were unattached, she'd never dreamed she'd made any impact on Michael Bradley whatsoever. He'd hidden his emotions, better even than her stoic brother.

"My attraction to you was unfair to the lady with whom I was supposed to be forming a lasting union," he added. "I had to call it off with her."

*Goodness!* He no longer seemed the cock-sure man she'd assumed him to be.

Then he smiled slightly. "Will you please do me the honor of sharing a meal, Elise?"

Her name on his tongue was as enticing as she'd imagined. It was downright sensual.

Without a second thought, she answered, "Yes, Michael. I will."

"Tomorrow night?" he asked.

She nodded, her thoughts briefly flitting to whether she would need a chaperone, and if so, whom.

"May I pick you up at seven at your home on Mount Vernon Street?"

She nodded again, and he stroked the side of her face so tenderly, she almost melted against him once more. But then he took a step back and reached past her to turn the bronze knob.

With the door open to the waiting room, he spoke in a professional tone. "I am pleased I could be of assistance, Miss Malloy."

"Thank you, Mr. Bradley," she said in her most no-nonsense voice in case anyone was observing them. Hopefully, her hair was not in utter disarray or her clothing rumpled by his embrace.

Elise left with the impression she was walking on fluffy clouds, and she did not remember her feet touching the bank floor tiles. As she was assisted into her carriage, however, a single thought came crashing down on her: *I'm still engaged to Jonathon Amory.*

*I have a date with an engaged woman,* Michael thought, staring at the scene outside his window as he watched her drive off before letting the wooden blinds fall back into place. Not just any woman, either. The one with whom he had been fervently hoping to spend time ever since he'd first laid eyes on her.

He remembered her coming into the bank with her father as if it were yesterday. She'd captivated him with her beauty and elegance, especially for someone so young. Yet it was the stimulating exchange he'd overheard between her and Oliver Malloy which had really caught his interest.

Her father explained things to her, not as one would to a bored or disinterested daughter but as to an equal. She'd listened attentively, asked intelligent questions, and given every indication of a superior mind. His eyes had followed her until she'd left the bank that day.

With a wince, Michael recalled how happy he'd been to run into her at the courthouse, especially after being told by one of his friends at the bank that Attorney Malloy was inquiring after his status. Unthinkingly, he'd rushed over to her like a clumsy puppy.

Even after all this time, he remembered how awful he'd felt watching her expression dissolve into one of horrified humiliation.

Even so, he'd been unable to get Elise out of his thoughts, although he had tried for the sake of his parents and their friends' kind daughter, whom his mother had always hoped he would marry. When Elise had again come into the bank, accompanying her widowed mother, he'd broken it off with Victoria that evening. He could not in good conscience be with one woman when he spent all of his time fantasizing about another.

A woman whom he'd finally, at long-last, kissed. His groin tightened at the memory. Indeed, he'd been unable to stop himself once he got close to her. It was as if she'd already agreed to be his. Her eyes drew him in, her lips were so damned soft, and she tasted like mint. Then there was the smell of her skin and her hair, like lilacs. He wanted to bury his face in her hair. She had more than lived up to his fantasy.

The only dark cloud was the fact she had so readily agreed to marry Amory. Michael had a feeling she would have gone through with it, too, if he hadn't made her face precisely what she was doing. She was a puzzlement, but one he had every intention of figuring out.

There was only one thing for Elise to do. She had to end the farce at once. She headed for the Amory mansion on Warren Street. Jonathon wasn't there, but old Mr. Amory was at home. Seizing the opportunity, she asked the maid to find out if he would meet with her.

After a few minutes' wait, he appeared, looking far older than she'd remembered, but she hadn't seen him out in public in half a decade.

Taking slow, painful-looking steps, he leaned heavily upon a black polished cane, which he thumped down onto the thick rug with each step he took. A large silver handle protruded from between his gnarled fingers.

Patiently and silently, she awaited his approach until he stood before her.

"Shall we sit, young lady?" And they did.

His voice creaked, but his eyes were bright and clear. "It has been many years since a Malloy was in my house," he began, and she knew then that he had no knowledge of her earlier visits. Most likely, he had no idea she was engaged to his son.

"You look like my Celia," was his second statement.

Elise vaguely remembered the man's exquisitely beautiful daughter who'd captivated Reed. In her recollection, she and Celia shared only a passing resemblance due to their dark hair. Nothing else.

"Thank you," she said.

"Shall I skip the pleasantries and ask why you're here and not your father?"

His words startled her, and she felt uncertain if he had all his faculties after all.

"My father is deceased, sir."

He paused, frowning slightly. "I'm sorry to hear it. A fine attorney and a fair man. In a heated moment, he knew how to keep his head."

He closed his eyes, and she wondered if he was done with her.

"Mr. Amory," she began, and his eyes snapped open.

"What do you need, Miss Malloy? I pay a monthly penalty for my daughter's indiscretion, for what she tried to do to your brother. It was *your* brother, correct?"

She nodded.

"He should have left her well-enough alone. What more can I do?"

Clearly, he didn't know the payments had stopped a year ago. That would indicate someone else, undoubtedly Jonathon, was handling the family's finances. Yet he'd given her the impression it was his father who'd stopped making the payments.

She wasn't sure whether to tell the elder Amory anything now. It was within her reach to pay off the loan herself, although she was unsure if that was what her father would have wanted.

All of a sudden, the parlor door burst open, and Jonathon came charging in. He stopped short at seeing his father and Elise in close quarters.

After a moment of catching his breath, his gaze going from her to the older Mr. Amory, into the surprised silence, Jonathon said, "The maid told me you were here, Miss Malloy."

"As you can see," she agreed. "I am."

"What do you mean by running in here like that?" his father scolded. "Bad manners, if you ask me. You might have frightened our guest."

"No, I'm fine," Elise said, standing up. "I was just leaving."

"But you haven't told me why you came, my dear." Mr. Amory looked at her with a curious stare.

Before she could respond, Jonathon approached his father. "Why don't you go take a nap, sir? I'll handle Miss Malloy."

*Handle her!* She felt insulted.

"Nonsense, I'm not tired," Mr. Amory protested, right before a huge yawn split the old man's face. "Hm, maybe just a short rest."

There was a moment of silence as he struggled to rise and then began his walk across the room. Elise also stood, ready to depart.

"It was a pleasure to see you, young lady," he said without turning. "Again, I'm sorry about your father."

"Thank you, Mr. Amory," Elise said to his hunched back.

After he had shuffled out, Jonathon checked the door behind him to make sure it was firmly closed. Then he stood before her, looking like as welcoming as a thundercloud.

"What can I do for you?"

"As it turns out, nothing," she said. "I came to tell you I won't marry you."

His left eye twitched, and a flash of emotion flickered across his face—frustration, exasperation.

"Was it something my father said?" he asked, sounding concerned. "I can assure you—"

She tilted her chin. "As I said, I came in order to call off our engagement in person. However, I just discovered your father knew nothing about the cessation of payments on the loan. Moreover, he didn't even know you and I were recently engaged. You lied to me on more than one count."

Jonathon Amory did not have the grace to look ashamed. Instead, he held her gaze a long, chilling moment until she felt uncomfortable, even threatened. Looking as though he were weighing his options, his jaw clenched when he seemed to come to some decision.

"I need a wife, in name at least, and I've decided you will suit."

Her mouth must have dropped open slightly for he laughed at her.

"Call it off and I will tell everyone how your father took out the loan to pay off my family. Your brother's name will be back in the gutter where it belongs for defiling my sister. And your father's name, as well, for lying about it."

"That's despicable," Elise said, although she could well see how the loan was damning evidence.

He folded his arms. "Marry me, and it all goes away."

"I don't need your money anymore," she said quietly. "I have the means to pay off the loan that your family ought to be paying."

"That makes me no never mind. I'll still ruin you if you go back on our agreement."

She thought the floor shifted slightly. "For God's sake, why?"

"As I said, a man in my position needs a wife. Otherwise, suspicions arise, some that are too close to the truth," he said evenly, leaving her wondering at his meaning.

In truth, she'd never seen Jonathon Amory about town in the company of a female. However, his next sentence confused the issue further: "And bedding you, quite frankly, is sweet revenge for all the anguish your brother caused."

She paled. Amory wanted to punish her in the most intimate way because Reed had had relations with his sister. What a monster!

"This is absurd. I will tell my brother of your wickedness and deceit."

"No, you won't." Jonathon took the seat his father had vacated, draped one long arm across the back and crossed his legs as if he hadn't a care in the world. He shook his head, making an exaggerated tut-tutting sound.

"The upstanding Reed Malloy, pinnacle of Boston's legal aristocracy, keeping his bastard child in France while its melancholy mother pines away for him. How cruel! How immoral!"

Her brain whirled, grasping at thoughts, trying to imagine a way out, a way in which her brother would never find out about the loan or come to any harm by Jonathon's vicious lies. Making Jonathon stay silent was the only answer.

"How do I know you won't try to ruin my brother even after you and I marry?"

"Why would I damage my wife's family's reputation? I ask you. Is that the action of a sane man?"

Was he sane and simply driven by bitter revenge? She thought there was a touch of madness to him.

Desperately wanting to postpone any damaging actions Jonathon might take, she murmured, "I must think on it."

His eyes narrowed. "Don't think too long, Elise."

Her name sounded like a snake's hiss when *he* said it.

"I intend to get our license tomorrow. The announcement will be in all the papers by week's end," he paused. "Or your brother's name will. I promise you."

Grim-faced, and without saying another word, she fled his presence.

# CHAPTER SIX

Once home, Elise went straight to her room, avoiding her mother and her sisters. Sitting on her bed, she considered her options. It was too late to tell Reed. He'd go straight to the Amory house, and then the whole scandal would blow up in his face.

Jonathon would ruin him, and gladly. She had no doubt the man would be vindictive. She was certain there was more than merely hard feelings about Reed and Celia's dalliance. There was professional jealousy involved, as well.

The community of lawyers was small enough that even Elise had heard of Jonathon's misstep a year earlier when he'd lost a case due to his lack of research, preparedness, and general incompetence. Reed had told her Jonathon lost many clients after that.

After she became his wife, who knew how far he would go? He might insist she ask Reed to go into practice with him. She chewed on her lower lip. What a predicament! There were two men to whom she wanted to turn for assistance, her father and her brother, but both were unavailable to her.

*Michael.* His name popped into her mind, followed quickly by his comely face. For a moment, she considered asking him for help. After all, he already knew about the loan and seemed to have a strong opinion of Jonathon Amory. However, she dismissed the thought just as quickly. What could Michael do that wouldn't jeopardize Reed's standing?

Before going to bed that night, Elise sat at her writing desk and pulled out a piece of crisp stationery. What to say to Michael? How to word it so he would believe her yet not think too badly of her? She couldn't bear the thought of his disapproval although she knew it would be all but impossible to keep his admiration.

After the wedding announcement was published, she could never look into Michael's eyes again. And she most certainly couldn't go to dinner with him the next evening.

*Dear Mr. Bradley,*

*I apologize for any inconvenience this missive may cause you as I know you will receive it the morning of our arranged dinner date. However, after due reflection, I must cancel.*

*I am at present irrevocably engaged to Mr. Amory. It would be unseemly for me to be out with you in public. Further, if you are laboring under any misconceptions regarding the possibility of an attachment between us, you must desist. There cannot be one.*

*As for any other disclosures from your bank, I would ask that you mail them to my attention. If business necessitates a family member's presence, I will send my sister Sophie in my place. I would ask you once again not to mention the loan to any member of my family. The debt will be settled shortly, either by myself or by Mr. Amory.*

*Sincerely,*
*Elise L. Malloy*

She read it over before folding it, sealing it, and putting it aside to give to the maid in the morning. It would be delivered to Michael as soon as the bank opened.

Elise spent a fitful night trying to think of a way out of her dilemma and eventually fell into a troubled sleep. When she awoke, she made sure the letter went out immediately. After breakfast, feeling on pins and needles at the idea of Michael reading her words and of how he might react, she decided a long walk was in order before the day became too warm.

After strolling along Mount Vernon Street, down Walnut, and across the Common, she eventually headed home via Charles Street. As she turned right at the corner toward her house, a carriage stopped beside her. The driver was none other than Michael Bradley.

"Miss Malloy, can you please wait a moment?"

So stunned by his unexpected appearance, she glanced around to see if anyone was watching. As the street was quiet, she nodded her acquiescence. In an instant, he was on the sidewalk blocking her path.

"What's the meaning of this?" he asked without preamble. He held her letter, fluttering open as if he'd held it upon his lap, perhaps even reading it, while driving his carriage.

"It's rather self-explanatory, I should think," she said, flustered by his vehemence.

"Can you possibly mean what you have written?" He looked perplexed and even annoyed. "You have changed your mind and will not have dinner with me?"

All at once, finding she could barely take a breath, let alone stay and speak with him, Elise dodged around his imposing form. Already, she felt the emotions welling up in her throat and choking her. Helpless against the squeezing of her heart, she had taken only a step when his hand on her arm stopped her.

"I am engaged," she reiterated as fiercely as she could, not looking at him. Breaking free, she continued along the sidewalk toward her house.

"You were engaged yesterday when you let me kiss you," he said to her rigid back, his voice remaining level, not raised yet clearly angry.

She spun quickly around. "How dare you speak of it out loud? You risk everything, sir."

"I am merely speaking the truth between us. Something has happened between yesterday and today." His voice softened. "Please, Elise, tell me what is wrong."

Could she tell him? No. She had gone over and over it in her mind. Without another word, turning away from his dear face, she began walking toward home once more.

"Elise," he called again.

"I am so sorry," she said without turning. What else could she say? Feeling foolish and heartbroken, she walked stiffly, but not without hearing him give an exasperated groan, nearly a growl. She felt the same way. The passionate creature inside her was growling with frustration—to be so close to this man with whom her heart was inexplicably, irrevocably connected, so close and yet to have to walk away.

Rose met her at the front door. "There was a man here to see you, a handsome one at that," her sister said with a grin. "The one from the Crowninshields' party."

Clearly, she was excited by the visit from a stranger, and Elise couldn't blame her.

Her sister watched her carefully for some sign of interest. "He was very pleasing to the eye," she added.

Elise barely nodded, unpinning her hat and removing her gloves, placing everything carefully on the letter table in the front hall. Apparently, Michael had sought her at home first.

"He wouldn't say what it was about," Rose continued. "He was very mysterious, and he said he would only speak with you."

Elise offered only silence. What did young Rose know of mysterious and eye-pleasing men? Too much, apparently!

Her sister frowned, wanting more of a reaction. "What do you make of it?"

Elise needed to put a stop to Rose's persistent needling interest. "Really, I couldn't say. Thank you for the message. I'll go ask Cook to put on the water for some coffee."

She hurried away from her. No need to tell Rose she'd already run into that particular man on the street. Such a disclosure would elicit a cross-examination of epic proportions. Elise would rather plead ignorance of the whole ordeal.

And she did so again when Rose mentioned the mysterious caller over the main course of their evening repast, the meal Elise should have missed if she'd been able to follow her heart and spend the evening with Michael. No wonder the food tasted like sawdust.

Reed looked at Rose. "What did he want?"

Rose gave an unladylike shrug. "He wouldn't give me a clue. He asked only for Elise Malloy, and then he said that no one else could help him."

Elise feigned intense interest in her roast beef and decided again to say nothing.

"That's strange," Reed said. "Are you sure he didn't want Mrs. E. Malloy and got the names mixed up?" he asked after another moment's consideration.

Rose laughed. "Oh, no. He didn't want Mama. He was quite certain he needed to speak with Miss Elise."

When Elise looked up, she found Reed, Rose, and even their mother staring at her.

Reed touched her hand, and she had to look at him. "Do you know what this is about?" he asked.

Taking a deep breath, she lied to her brother for the first time in her life. "No idea." Then she went back to eating, feeling if possible, more miserable than she had earlier.

Their mother put down her wine glass. "Reed, dear, perhaps you should go to the bank tomorrow and find out. He's from the Massachusetts National, you know."

"No," Elise said more loudly and forcefully than she intended. She'd rather hoped her mother had forgotten about the man who'd cradled her in his arms at the party. She, herself, had certainly not remembered introducing them.

All eyes again regarded her with interest. Even Sophie, who'd been studying a musical score that lay beside her dinner plate, now stared at her. Reed's eyebrows shot up quizzically, and she knew she had to finesse this quickly or he would be on her like the astute lawyer he was.

"What I mean is if the man came here to see me, then I should be the one to find out why." She turned to her mother. "This isn't the turn of the century, Mother. I'm quite capable of going to the bank. Besides, it may have been a simple mistake, and it would be a waste of Reed's time. He's very busy."

Reed gave his sister an extra-long look before turning to their mother. "I couldn't go tomorrow, in any case. Court is in session." He ran his fingers through his hair. "Perhaps the following day if Elise has not sorted it out by then. I'm sorry not to be of more use, but I'm sure she can handle whatever it is." He gave his older sister a broad wink of encouragement.

"I suppose," their mother said. "But let us know if you need help, dear."

Elise rolled her eyes. If her mother only knew. Still, she breathed a sigh of relief. Her brother must, indeed, be distracted by work, or he would have caught on to her slight agitation and interrogated her all the rest of the evening.

She would have to come up with some reason why the bank had sent Michael to their house. But for the life of her, at that moment, she couldn't think of a single plausible purpose to his visit. And perhaps more urgently, she needed to make sure he did not come to their home again.

The next day, she waited until the bank closed, at four o'clock sharp. Despite a sudden summer shower that she staved off with her carriage's hood, Elise boldly parked a block from the bank's front door, holding her horse's reins. She waited with an uncomfortably clenched stomach for Michael.

When he appeared, her heartbeat sped up to an alarming rate, and her head felt instantly light. She couldn't believe she was being so outrageously, unable to fathom she was actually approaching him in such a manner.

He had a newspaper over his bare head, no hat or umbrella in sight, and he was hurrying in the opposite direction. She flicked the reins, and her horse moved forward. Drawing the carriage beside him, she said, "Mr. Bradley, a word, please."

He looked up at her, his face a picture of astonishment, and he stopped dead in his tracks.

"Are you toying with me?" he asked her, sounding strangely defeated.

"I assure you, I am not," she said, hardly able to hear herself over the rain and her loudly beating heart. "I would speak privately with you a moment. Please."

He glanced around. There was barely anyone on the street due to the downpour.

"Why didn't you come into the bank?" he asked, one of his hands resting on her front wheel as if he intended to keep her there. He had lowered his newspaper, and the rain was dripping off his hat brim, onto his shoulders and under his collar, but he didn't seem to notice. She shivered.

He *knew* why she hadn't gone into the bank. She was sure he had guessed. She couldn't go into his office in such close quarters where the closed door afforded them too much privacy, too much temptation.

She only shook her head.

"Very well," he said, "However, I refuse to stand here getting soaked a moment longer." His tone was clipped and angry. Without warning, he climbed up onto the small dickey and took the reins out of her gloved hands.

"Goodness!" she exclaimed.

Michael said nothing. With a twitch of the reins, he caused her horse to amble slowly down the street. Elise stayed silent. This would be the only time in her life she would ride beside Michael Bradley, and it felt heavenly. His leg pressed against hers, warm despite his clothes being damp, her shoulder leaned into his arm, which felt comfortingly solid.

She was tingling from head to toe and nearly closed her eyes to better experience it, but she didn't want to miss a moment.

*What if someone she knew saw them?* The dreadful thought sliced into her mind. She would be compromised, if not ruined. Then she relaxed. She would say her horse was giving her trouble, and this kind banker whom her father had known offered to assist her home.

Except they couldn't go to her home to talk. She was about to tell him so when it became apparent they weren't going to Beacon Hill at all. Instead, he drove to the newer development of Back Bay. After a few more minutes, he steered her little carriage behind a row of tidy houses and into the back alley where carriages were parked and horses were stabled.

In moments, a groom popped out of a small carriage house and took hold of her horse's bridle as Michael climbed down from the seat. Turning, he held his hand up to her.

Elise hesitated. Yet compelled by his forthright expression, she let him help her down and escort her inside the dwelling by the back entrance.

It was positively silent inside the small mudroom, and despite the earliness of the evening hour, it was also dark due to the rain clouds overhead.

Stopping short in the gloom, Elise waited, wondering how on earth she'd ended up there. Michael followed her in, eased around her, and then faced her.

"Will you come all the way inside?" he asked, gesturing to the open doorway leading to a long passage, also unlit.

"Where is your help?" she asked, not taking a step forward.

He shrugged. "My servants don't live here. A cleaning woman comes in every other day, and when I need a meal prepared, another lady comes to cook. I am usually out or at my parents' home. It didn't seem worthwhile to maintain a staff for only myself."

It was a long explanation to say that they were alone. She took a breath. This was obviously another level of outrageousness that could never have occurred to her. That she, Elise Malloy, would be alone in a man's house! She hoped her father wasn't watching.

"You wanted to speak privately," he reminded her, taking a single step and reaching out his hand as if to take hers.

She ignored his gesture, keeping her hands firmly clasped in front of her. Walking past him, she continued along the hallway. Having spent time in similar homes belonging to her parents' friends, she knew the layout of the townhouse instinctively.

Toward the anterior of the foyer by the main door, she went into the parlor on the right.

Michael watched her walk down the hallway of his home, and he knew he would do anything to make this a common occurrence, an everyday one in fact, and to keep her for himself.

It was easy to imagine her as his wife, his mate for the rest of his life, bringing her beauty and her woman's touch to his home. He could not lose her to whatever was pulling her away from him.

Following her, he ducked his head around the corner to see her standing in the middle of his sitting room, looking surprised to be there and not at all relaxed.

"Would you like a cup of coffee?" he offered.

For a moment, she only stared at him, her intense blue eyes showing alarm. Perhaps because there were no safeguards of bank customers or office staff outside the door, perhaps because of his personal knowledge that she would have grimaced if he'd offered her tea.

In any case, she refused. "Nothing, thank you. Let's talk, Mr. Bradley, and then, I should go."

So, she was back to "Mr. Bradley." Well, he could remedy that. Approaching her before she knew what he was doing, he slipped his arms around her slender waist and lowered his head to her stunned face.

"I am going to kiss you," he told her a second before he did. Her hands reached up to press against his chest, perhaps to push him away. However, when his mouth touched hers and as he slanted his lips to fit her mouth more perfectly, she relaxed.

Her hands stopped warding him off and began grasping at his suit coat, holding him in place. She needn't have bothered. He wasn't going anywhere, unless it was upstairs to his bedroom with her.

He smiled against her lips at that wild thought and felt her smile, too.

This was so precisely right, he wondered how they could have gone so long without doing it before yesterday.

Many moments later, he lifted his mouth from hers. He needed to see her lovely blue eyes framed by thick ebony lashes. She had a delightfully soft pink blush to her cheeks. He couldn't help himself as he bent to kiss her again.

"Michael," she said, the word coming out on a gasp for breath. "You must stop. *We* must stop. This is wrong."

"Yet impossibly perfect," he added.

She sighed. "Maybe so, if it were simply the two of us. Alone," she began.

"But we are alone—"

"I mean, alone forever, without consequences, but we're not. And you're wet," she added.

She was correct. Stepping away from her, he slipped off his damp coat and tossed it over a chair, then shook his hair like a dog and ran his fingers through it.

"Probably not so neat," he said, "but not dripping on you anymore either."

He took her in his arms again, leaning away so he could watch her face while keeping her in his embrace.

"How can our love—?" he broke off as he felt her startle at his words, and he nearly laughed. "Yes, *love*, for I swear I am unreservedly and wholly in love with you, Elise Malloy, and have been from the moment I first met you. I want to shout it." And he did. He tipped his head back and yelled, "I love Elise Malloy."

His words echoed slightly in the empty three-story townhouse.

Her eyes were as large as saucers, but she didn't look scared of his enthusiastic outburst. In fact, she seemed amused by his antics.

"I think you feel the same way?" he conjectured.

She looked down at his chest but nodded ever so slightly.

That small gesture, her admission of having the same feelings for him, caused a flood of warmth to cascade through him. And relief.

"I ask you, then," he said, tipping her chin up so he could look into her eyes, "how can our love have consequences that are anything but good? How are *we* wrong?"

"Mr. Amory—"

"Don't speak to me of that ninny. You already told me you don't even like him. Just tell him, 'thank you, you damned puffed peacock of a mediocre attorney, but no thank you'. Or tell him to go to hell. I don't care."

"I can't," she said, her voice a miserable whisper.

He wanted to make her smile again, but he had a feeling a simple kiss wouldn't do.

"Why not? You have feelings for me, even if you can't quite declare them aloud. I can tell when I look in your eyes or whenever I'm close enough to touch you."

Her cheeks reddened.

"You don't deny it?" he urged her.

She shook her head. "No, but I'm afraid I have a situation on my hands. Jonathon Amory refuses to let me go."

"The hell he won't," he said before he could stop himself.

She jumped at his tone, and he was immediately sorry to have frightened her. However, he'd felt his own flash of fear at her words. They sounded so final, as if she were already Amory's wife, and there was nothing he or she or anyone could do about it.

"Explain what you mean. How can he refuse to let you go?"

"Blackmail," she said.

# CHAPTER SEVEN

Elise's eyelids swept closed, shutting him out as she hung her head low. However, before she did so, he had seen tears. Michael led her to the settee.

"Sit," he ordered and watched her sink down onto the cushions.

At the sideboard, he poured them both a glass of red Spanish wine. Holding a glass out to her, he waited. She lifted her gaze to him, an eyebrow raised.

"I'm not trying to make you inebriated, Elise. I've seen how addled you can become, and right now, I want you entirely clear-headed, but I also want you to relax and tell me what's going on."

She took the glass and held it against her chest, shivering slightly. Placing his own glass on the low table in front of the sofa, he checked the iron stove in the hearth for coal and, finding it full, lit it. Despite it being summer, that afternoon was unseasonably chilly.

"My apologies for letting you stand in this cold room. When I'm with you, I tend not to think about anything else except holding you."

She gave a slight laugh behind him, although the sound still held the threat of tears. He clenched his jaw. He would get it all out of her tonight, whatever it was, and they would face it together.

After drawing the curtains, he lit the gas lamps. The room became cozy and welcoming, and the soft glow of the flickering lamps bathed her, making her look like a raven-haired angel. He took a seat beside her on the sofa, noting she'd taken a few sips of wine before putting the glass down.

"Feeling better?" he asked her profile, as she looked toward the glass window in the iron stove and not at him.

"Yes, I'm warmer inside and out, but not any closer to a solution."

"Then let's work on that," he said. "Solutions are my specialty." He knew he sounded idiotic, but he couldn't help himself. He would do anything to erase her sadness.

She turned to him, her gaze locking with his.

"As you already know, the loan statements were being sent to the Amory house. After my father died, apparently Jonathon took it upon himself to stop making payments even though his father thinks they are still being made."

She paused and looked so doleful he put his arm around her and pulled her to him. Letting her lay her head on his chest, he rested his chin on her head. It felt like the most natural thing in the world.

"Do you want to tell me why your father took out a loan for the Amorys?" He felt her sigh.

"It was a nasty bit of business that involved Mr. Amory's daughter and my brother, but I don't wish to say more, and I most certainly don't want Reed to know anything about this."

She lifted her hand and absentmindedly stroked his ribs, causing every nerve in his body to catch fire.

Catching his breath, he held it until the sensation subsided, trying to remain focused on her words. Easy as it would be to get carried away with her, he genuinely wanted to help.

"Suffice it to say," Elise continued, unmindful of what torture she was putting him through with her nearness and her gentle touch, "Reed was in danger of being sorely taken advantage of. My father stepped in to help."

Michael had another question for her, and he wished there was a delicate way to ask it.

"Do I understand correctly that you do not have the money to pay back the loan, and you're marrying Amory so he'll pay it off?"

Even as he asked, it sounded tawdry and beneath her, but he supposed a woman in a desperate situation could act accordingly. He felt her stiffen, and then she pushed away from him and stood up. Instantly, he regretted even asking.

"That's insulting." Elise started to pace. "This started out as a ridiculous prevarication. I intentionally lied to you in your office out of embarrassment when I said I had a beau. I intended to produce one at the party. I had my sights set on Mr. Nickerson."

"Nickerson," Michael sputtered, as he was sipping the wine. "*Old* Mr. Nickerson?"

"Kind, sweet Mr. Nickerson," she amended. "It would have been merely for one evening."

He shook his head. If only he hadn't been so rash as to try to compel her into going out with him. If only he'd known she was amenable to the idea.

"Then Jonathon asked me to marry him out of the blue at your uncle's home, right before the dancing started."

She stopped and stared at him, her eyes so passionate and stunning.

"Suddenly, you were approaching across the Crowninshields' ballroom, and I was . . . slightly in my cups." She dipped her head. "I told Jonathon 'yes' impulsively. I could see you didn't believe me right from the start."

"That's because a few days earlier, you'd had no idea who lived at that address when you first came to me, so I knew he wasn't really your suitor."

She held up her hand. "I regretted it immediately. Well, almost. Especially when I figured out how to pay off the loan without my family having to ever know about it."

"Do tell," he said.

"Why are you smiling?" she asked instead.

"Because you are so damn beautiful, I can't stand it. And because I knew you would be resourceful enough to figure a way out of your dilemma."

"I was in possession of a fifteenth-century translation of the *History of Troy.*" She paused. "By William Caxton."

He whistled. "That must be worth quite a pretty penny."

She nodded.

"You said 'was in possession'?"

"I sold it. I have more than enough to pay off the loan."

Yet Michael watched her face fall.

"Then why do you look so miserable, Elise?"

She swallowed, and when she did speak, it came out in a throaty whisper, "He says I must marry him or he'll ruin Reed's reputation."

Michael stood up, watching her as she crossed her arms around her waist protectively.

"He threatened to drag my brother's name through the mud, even though what he will say are lies. He said the very fact of my father being so generous and taking out that loan for the Amorys will be proof enough." She looked at him, her blue eyes stormy. "I can't let my brother suffer."

"You would marry Amory to protect Reed?"

She didn't hesitate, "I would."

With her answer, he fell even more in love with her. What would it be like to have the love and devotion of such a woman?

Michael moved carefully around the table, which he felt like kicking to smithereens, but not as much as he wanted to smash Amory's face. He took her hands.

"I will not let you marry that bastard. Even if I wasn't in love with you. Even if I didn't already consider you my own. No woman should marry him."

"Why?" she asked.

"He doesn't really want a wife, or a woman, for that matter." He hesitated to say more.

She frowned. "But then why did he . . . ?" She trailed off, looking stricken.

"Why did he what?" he asked.

"Vow to bed me to punish my brother."

Michael clenched his jaw and had to calm down before he spoke. So incensed that anyone would seek to harm this lovely creature in front of him, he felt his neck grow hot and his collar feel tight, thinking his head might explode if he didn't get his anger under control. She watched the pulse of his jawline, and he took a deep breath to calm himself.

"Amory probably would have done so, too, but only for that reason and to get an heir."

Elise nodded. "He mentioned wanting an heir."

*Son of a bitch!* "Forget about Amory," he said, telling himself as much as he was telling her. "You are mine. An engagement announcement, rings, a license, even a wedding—at this moment, they all seem like delays and unimportant obstacles. Formalities, if you will. I already feel as though you belong to me, Elise Malloy. Am I insane?"

She pulled one hand free of his and put it up to his cheek. "I asked my father to find out if you were otherwise attached that day because the first time I saw you, I knew you were the man I wanted for my own."

Michael captured her hand and turned to kiss her palm. He knew it was wrong at this moment when she was in anguish over Amory, but he felt himself stir and grow hard. He wanted to carry her upstairs, or even to the sofa, and make love to her.

Before long, someday soon, he knew he would peel away every layer of her clothing and kiss every inch of her skin's velvety softness. When he fit himself between her legs and moved inside her, he wanted to watch her dark blue eyes widen at the precise instant of their joining. Then he intended to make them grow misty and unfocused with pleasure.

He could hardly wait to please her. It was inevitable.

"You don't have to marry Amory. I can, in fact, solve your problem."

Dizziness stormed Elise's senses as she experienced a moment of sheer relief. Then it dissipated, replaced once more by doubt and the impossibility of silencing Jonathon Amory. She shook her head.

"That's impossible."

Michael's hands slipped into her hair in the space below her small jaunty hat, cradling her head, and his lips took hers, stealing her breath and her thoughts until there was no worry over Reed's future or fear of Jonathon's reprisals, no loan, nor insidious blackmail. Only Michael. The man who lived in her heart.

"Not impossible," he said, against her mouth.

He nibbled on her lower lip, sending waves of tingling sensations right to her womanly core. When his insistent tongue demanded entrance, she opened her mouth and welcomed him in. Had she just moaned? Or were her ears playing tricks on her?

Her hands, almost of their own accord, laced together behind his neck, and her body answered his like a siren call. She pressed against him.

How would they ever get through a conversation when they were locked together every few minutes? What a life it would be if he were hers, to live with this man, always anticipating the next time she would be in his arms.

Cautiously, timidly at first, she traced her tongue along the side of his and felt his body shudder. Emboldened by her power, she did it again, and this time, she knew the moan came from him.

His arms tightened around her back and somehow, she was crushed even closer, her breasts flattened against his chest, her nipples throbbing to life along with the rest of her. She understood what he meant by the trappings of an engagement and a wedding being merely formalities. If she could go against the ingrained morals of her upbringing, she would give herself to him that very night.

The next moment, he lifted her into his arms. She gasped.

"Let me take you to bed," he murmured, his voice husky, sending shivers down her spine. The word *bed* from his lips seemed like the most debauched, sensual word in the entire world. He carried her toward the door.

It would be beyond easy to give in. She could imagine being immersed in the passion cresting between them. It would be so utterly simple to succumb to the temptation of his warmth and his offer of love.

Instead, she grabbed the door trim when he skirted the doorway, and rather ungracefully, she pulled him to a halt.

"No," she said.

He froze, and she could feel his heart beating fast in his chest. "No?" he asked.

"No. Please, Michael, put me down."

She felt him hesitate, even sigh. Then he lowered her to the ground with only a muttered "Blast it all!"

Straightening her clothing, tugging down her fitted jacket, and making certain her hat was still pinned properly, she tried to steady her breathing and slow her pulse. Imagine if she'd let him take her up the stairs and into his room. Imagine undressing in front of his watchful green-flecked brown eyes. Imagine the feel of his fingers stroking her bare skin.

"Elise."

"Yes?" She felt as though she was in a dream.

"If you make another soft moaning sound like that, I'm going to pick you up again."

Had she moaned while merely imagining him loving her?

"I cannot start something with you—"

"Too late," Michael interrupted. "We're well past the start, as far as I'm concerned."

He sounded a tad uncertain, so she nodded in agreement but couldn't help wringing her hands to keep from touching him.

"Very well. I cannot *continue* something with you," she amended, "not while I'm embroiled in this terrible situation with—"

He held up his hand. "Please, stop saying his godforsaken name." He tucked a wisp of her hair behind her ear. "Come. Let's at least scare up some dinner while I tell you how I plan to rescue you, dear lady. I believe I have cheese at least and a loaf of bread, maybe some kind of pickled vegetable. Either onions or cauliflower, perhaps."

She stared at him. Truly? He wanted to eat at such a juncture. Pickled cauliflower and savory cheese? Then she realized she was, indeed, hungry.

"All right," she said. "I'll bring our wine."

Returning to his sitting room, she picked up their half-full glasses. Strangely, she felt at home as if she'd been there before. Retracing her steps to the back of the house, she found the kitchen where Michael was already spreading out food on a central work table.

He pulled up a stool, no doubt what his cook used were she to sit and peel potatoes or apples. He gestured for her to sit upon it.

"Sit and listen," he told her.

And she did.

# CHAPTER EIGHT

"Stop it, Mother. I'm a grown woman," Elise said, swinging her legs over the side of the bed and getting up while Evelyn Malloy fretted, and quite loudly, too, about the scandalous behavior of her eldest daughter.

Her mother put her hands to her own cheeks in dismay, rolling her eyes with exasperation, and then she shook her head.

"You came home very late last night. You missed dinner! And I still don't know where you were or why."

"I'm sorry to have worried you, but please, calm yourself." Thank goodness her mother didn't know where she'd been before her evening ride home. How quietly Elise had attempted to slip into the house, yet of course, her mother had caught her as she'd entered from the small back garden after taking their horse and carriage into the alley behind.

Silently and with a forbidding face, her mother had pointed to the staircase, and Elise had dutifully ascended, trying to look chastised, well aware a scene of interrogation would occur in the morning. Regardless, she'd slept soundly knowing Michael was truly her knight, like Sir Galahad. And happily for her, he was far more earthly and much less angelic than the famed knight.

A smile stole across her face, merely thinking of him and of their dinner and their long conversation afterward by the warm stove. It had been difficult to come home at all. And then her early morning musings were shattered by her mother storming into her room before breakfast.

Elise sighed. What she needed was a lock on her door! No, what she actually needed was to be Michael's wife and move into his house and start a blissfully wedded life.

"If you won't answer *my* questions, perhaps your brother can get it out of you," her mother continued. "Well-bred young ladies do not go out unaccompanied at half past three in the afternoon in inclement weather, and they certainly do not come at midnight."

"So, if the weather had been fine?" Elise asked impertinently.

"That is not the point," Evelyn said, "and you know it."

"I came home hours before midnight," Elise insisted. "And please, do not bother Reed. This is none of his concern." She raised an eyebrow in the way her brother did. "He is *not* my father."

She watched her mother accept it and then purse her lips. Elise knew she'd won but hated to cause her mother any distress.

"Please, Mama, don't worry. Everything will be fine." She stared deeply into her mother's lovely verdant eyes. "Trust me. I am *your* daughter, after all."

Evelyn relaxed slightly. "So is Rose, and you see what mischief she gets up to," she said, but she offered a small smile.

"True," Elise acknowledged. "Maybe all the good sense was used up on myself and Reed and Sophie." She reached out and squeezed her mother's hand.

"Very well," Evelyn gave in. "For now, I will let this matter drop, but I will want some answers. And soon. You promise you're not in any trouble?"

Elise caught her breath. Why were mothers so uncannily knowing? She'd nearly been in a world of trouble, but she hoped today, she would be getting out of it completely.

"I promise, Mother." Michael would see to it.

A few hours later, she gave Michael her hand, and he assisted her down from his phaeton in front of the Amorys' Warren Street mansion.

She'd made sure Jonathon would be home before she met Michael at the bank and left her carriage there.

"Don't worry," he said, his hand warming the small of her back.

"Actually, I'm not." She felt confident with Michael by her side, believing she could do anything.

They were shown into the parlor where Jonathon Amory sat, legs crossed, reading the paper, drinking tea.

*Infernal tea,* she thought.

As she expected, his father was nowhere to be seen. She had a nasty feeling Jonathon kept the older gentleman locked away from society.

And why was Jonathon nearly always at home while her brother was busy at all hours working at the courthouse or the law library at Dane? Didn't he have any cases at present?

As Jonathon's glance registered Michael, he paled, and Elise knew with certainty everything would be all right.

"I was expecting you alone, Elise," he said, lowering his paper.

"You will address her properly, befitting your relationship," Michael said, outwardly bristling as he moved to stand with one leg slightly in front of her skirts. "She is Miss Malloy to you, Amory. And you will show her all due respect and stand in her presence."

Elise knew they'd better wrap this up as quickly as possible. She could feel the anger emanating from Michael like heat from his cast iron stove, and she had a feeling he was not going to be civil for long.

"I beg your pardon," Jonathon said, finally rising slowly, but he was not begging forgiveness. Rather, he was clearly questioning Michael's proprietary stance.

"Beg all you like," Michael muttered, turning his head away. "It'll do you no good."

"Mr. Amory," Elise began, "it has come to my attention that ours would be a marriage in name only." She glanced pointedly at Michael as the source of this information.

Dark blotches, from either anger or trepidation, put the color back in Jonathon's cheeks. She thought his mouth dropped slightly. Then he straightened.

"How dare you!"

"This question from a blackmailer," Michael remarked. "How ironic!" He let that outrageously bold statement hang in the air a moment before he added, "You will cease in your persecution of Miss Malloy and her family. At once."

Beside her, Michael appeared relaxed, yet she knew how his anger simmered at what Jonathon was trying to do to her.

For his part, Jonathon looked down his nose at them both, as if a dead fish resided at the end of it. "Or what? I am an attorney. I'll bring the full extent of the law against you for slander if you so much as whisper your insinuations."

Elise sighed. He was a fool to think he could scare her with such talk. She'd heard her father and brother banter such statements about enough times to know it was a last resort defense for the defenseless. Before Michael had a chance, she answered him.

"I will tell everyone of your inclination toward your own gender. Personally, I care not a whit about that or about what you do in private, but I do not wish to be married to you, and I will do whatever I must to stop you from pressuring me."

"You are playing with fire," Jonathon said, although without the force of his previous statement.

"No, Amory," Michael snapped back. "You are. I heard you plainly and clearly proposition a young clerk inside the bank. What was it, about three months past? No matter. I'll ask him to corroborate the precise date if you like. This is not hearsay. This is, as you know, first-person evidence of the most damning nature."

Michael took a step toward Jonathon who appeared mute with rage, and Elise reached out her hand, thinking to restrain Michael from harming him. However, he glanced at her and gave a curt shake of his head.

She understood, dropping her arm at once. Men were men, and while Michael loved and respected her, she had better not think to get between them, any more than she'd try to separate two growling dogs.

"I will crucify you in court," Michael continued, "and I won't need the help of a lawyer to do it. You are free to live your life however you see fit, and I could not possibly care less about such matters, until you attempt harm, as you are doing now. So, I will say this again and only once more. You will leave the lady alone, and you will not bother her or her family again."

Elise couldn't help adding, "I don't even need you to pay off the loan. I simply want no further contact. Do you agree?"

Jonathon Amory stood unmoving, looking from her to Michael. He said nothing else on the matter. At last, he nodded.

Elise felt a weight lift from her shoulders. "I must have your word that you will do nothing to harm my brother. You must accept that Celia was at fault, and my family has been generous regarding the matter."

"Get out," Jonathon said, all veneer of civility vanished from his countenance.

"Your word," Elise insisted, even as Michael turned and took her arm to urge her out.

"What is that worth?" Michael asked her, not caring if Amory heard or not. As far as he was concerned, Amory's claws had been snipped.

She let Michael steer her toward the door, but thought she might have heard Jonathon murmur, "You have it."

"Where are we going now?" Elise asked him, feeling as if she could fly like a chickadee. She was free, free from the worry over paying off the loan, free from Jonathon Amory, free to love Michael Bradley.

"Back to the bank," he said. "You're going to climb into your carriage and go home."

"Oh," she felt slightly let down. She'd expected something far more extraordinary after the exciting past twenty-four hours they'd shared.

"I'll be there shortly," he added, "and we'll talk to Reed together."

Michael was coming to her house? She could interpret that in only one way, and it rendered her silent.

"I must to speak to your brother immediately about our getting married."

"And my mother," she added.

He nodded. "Of course. And your mother."

Leaning her cheek against his shoulder, Elise smiled to herself. Oliver Malloy's taking out that generous loan had led to her uniting with Michael at last, and she would consider it her father's last gift.

Later, when Michael sat with her entire family, Rose and Sophie included, and told them how he had held her in high esteem since first meeting her over two years earlier, she couldn't help beaming.

"When I am with Miss Malloy," Michael added, seated opposite and staring directly at her, "I feel as if I'm in the company of an ever-present, densely saturated goodness."

Elise blushed at such grandiloquent words about herself, and in front of her open-mouthed siblings and her mother. Yet inside her soft leather shoes, she wiggled her toes with pleasure.

Reed looked from one to the other. "And this sudden decision to marry was made when precisely?"

Elise smiled. Her brother managed to look serious and paternal despite being younger than either her or Michael. However, more than that, she knew he was pondering recent events and trying to determine if he'd missed something. His legally trained mind was searching for clues and coming up with . . . nothing.

Michael coughed and cleared his throat. "I apologize for speaking with Miss Malloy first regarding marriage. However, after we discovered we had a mutual admiration, I spoke plainly with her."

The look he sent her, causing her to catch her breath and glance away, was a reminder they'd done more than *speak* plainly.

"Reed," Elise said firmly, "stop interrogating my future husband."

Standing, she walked from her chair to the sofa where Michael sat sandwiched between her sisters. Pushing between him and Rose, who was clearly fascinated by the turn of events, Elise sat close and took his hand.

"For make no mistake, dear family," she said, glancing at her mother and brother in the matching wingchairs, "I intend to marry him."

# EPILOGUE

In Michael's bedroom, now hers, too, lit only by the fireplace and a few flickering candles, Elise stood in the center of a rich blue and gold Persian rug. Wrapped in nothing but a white silken robe, she tied the belt loosely at her waist.

Feeling not a tremor of fear, instead she relished the distinct trembling of anticipation.

Her fiancé had waited impatiently for two weeks to become her husband, which was the least amount of time in which they could get married without appearing in an unsuitable hurry after the announcement was made. Of course, Reed made sure their marriage license was in order.

For the seemingly interminable duration, Michael had paced and fumed, held her hand every time they were close, and kissed her thoroughly every time they were alone.

Finally, it was their wedding night, after a perfect, small service with only his family and her family.

Her new husband had gone downstairs to see the cook out and to lock up their house.

Already bathed in a tub of scented lilac water, Elise took down her thick, dark hair and carefully brushed it out. Now she waited, trying not to appear like a sacrificial virgin. Rather, she wanted to be exactly who she was, an eager wife who was ready to please her husband and be pleased by him.

Michael pushed the door open slowly, leaving him silhouetted against the dark hallway.

"There's my gorgeous bride." Barely pausing to take in her appearance, he entered the room and swiftly took her in his arms.

She relaxed into his embrace, totally comfortable and utterly in love with this man.

"I can't believe you're my husband."

He smiled. "You're supposed to let *me* say that. I am astounded you are my wife, Elise Malloy Bradley, the most beautiful woman in all of Boston."

Tugging at his waistcoat buttons, she suddenly felt a little shy. "You don't have to flatter me. I'm yours already."

"Flattery is for fools," Michael stated. "I am speaking the truth." He paused, gazing into her eyes, his face so dear to her. "But you are mine in name and heart only."

While she started to protest his use of the word *only*, he lowered his head and kissed her. She knew the moment his demeanor changed from earnest love to passionate desire. His hands moved from her waist, sliding down her hips before curling under her bottom.

Pulling her tightly against him, fitting her against his lean hips, at the same time, he trailed kisses along her jawline and down the pale curve of her neck.

She arched her neck and immediately, his hand came up to cradle her head. His other hand was at her belt, untying and nudging open her robe. Shutting her eyes as his mouth moved lower, his lips skimmed her collar bone before coming to rest upon her left breast, directly over her fast-beating heart.

She gasped as Michael's mouth closed over her tightly pearled nipple. How long he feasted there, Elise didn't know. Her body was exploding with new and exciting sensations, her brain felt drugged with pleasure, and there was nothing in the world but him and her.

"Now, dear wife, I'm going to make you mine in another way."

He lifted her off her feet and gently deposited her in the middle of his—*their*—bed.

She opened her eyes to watch him undress, wondering at her inability to breathe deeply.  A part of her wanted to laugh, simply to dissipate the built-up tension. At the same time, she savored the flutter of excitement low in her belly, and the pulsing need at the apex of her thighs.

Shoes, vest, suspenders, starched collar, shirt. He paused, and she enjoyed her first unfettered view of his naked upper body, with his nicely formed shoulders over strong arms that made her feel safe and protected. His chest, broad and flat, had a smattering of curly hair she couldn't wait to touch, and his lean stomach held interesting indentations of muscle over his ribs, before his torso ended in a gentle narrowing down to his hips and beneath the waist of his trousers.

She swallowed. All this maleness was hers, and there was more to come.

"You're beautiful," she murmured, rising up, resting upon her elbows, not caring that her robe gaped open and exposed her breasts.

He laughed, which she liked. "No, I'm not," he insisted. "*You're* beautiful."

Then he came to stand beside the bed. Slipping his hand into the opening of her gown, he palmed her left breast, before rubbing his thumb over her pert nipple.

"Oh," she gasped. It seemed as though all of her senses were focused on that one small bud as he played with it.

And then he did the same to her other breast, and for a moment, she closed her eyes, letting the new sensations overtake her. When his hands roamed lower, pushing her gown open entirely, she couldn't contain a small moan. Her eyelids snapped open to watch. Looking down at her own body, she was mesmerized by the sight of his fingers trailing along her smooth stomach toward the place that longed for his touch, even then growing damp with desire.

She gasped again as he touched the curls between her legs.

"You are so very beautiful," he whispered, his tone grown husky.

Her gaze flicked up to his face, amazed to see a reflection of her own raw and deep feelings etched there. She said nothing as he stroked and caressed her most intimate place until her hips were lifting off the bed to meet his touch, her body wanting more—until she could nearly weep with the pleasure. And still, he hadn't yet come to bed!

She stilled his hand, capturing it under her own and taking in a few ragged breaths.

"Very well. You're *handsome*," she amended, sighing with sheer delight, unable to imagine being happier than she was at that moment with her new husband undressing before her. "Yet truly, I do think you're beautiful, too."

He shook his head, a wicked grin on his face. "I wonder how you will describe the rest of me."

The easy smile was wiped from her face as he began to unfasten his pants. Holding her breath, she watched his every move until, at last, he stood stark naked, clenching and unclenching his fists by his sides, appearing slightly tentative under her intense scrutiny.

"I think I'm going to like this whole husband and wife arrangement," she said at last, breaking the anxious moment.

Collapsing back onto the bed, she spread her arms wide. In an instant, Michael had climbed onto the mattress and was settling over her willing body, skin to heated skin. She looked up at him expectantly.

"I love you, Mrs. Bradley," he said. Then he held her face still with his large, gentle fingers while he proceeded to ravage her mouth with his own.

When he let her breathe again, delighting in the feeling of her husband's bare chest rasping across her own rising and falling breasts, she answered him.

"I love you, too, Mr. Bradley. Now, hurry up and make me yours in this other way."

And he did, for much of the night and for the rest of their lives.

*The End*

A stranger arrives from Boston seeking Miss Charlotte Sanborn. Before long, Charlotte is riding a train heading east toward high society, delicious romance, and perilous intrigue.

*Turn the page for an excerpt from*

# *An* Improper Situation

## DEFIANT HEARTS BOOK 1

# Sydney Jane Baily

# CHAPTER ONE

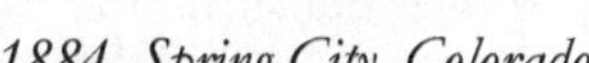

*1884, Spring City, Colorado*

Charlotte heard the wagon wheels and the horse's hooves from where she sat at her desk, and a frown crossed her otherwise clear features.

"Blazes!" she exclaimed. She was not expecting anyone. Moreover, except for Sarah Cuthins, the doctor's wife, Charlotte and her other neighbors weren't, well, neighborly enough with each other for uninvited visits. And she could tell just by listening that it wasn't Sarah's buggy coming down the dirt road.

Anyway, she couldn't see who it was even if she tried to look out the window, as books were piled high in front of it. Books were, in fact, the dominant feature in the study—on history, modern and ancient languages, classical architecture, mathematics, even oceanology, entomology, and geology.

In the middle of them all, Charlotte sat at her large desk, which had once been her father's. Currently, and always in fact, newspapers and other papers were strewn across it. A faded globe perched precariously on one corner, a lamp on another.

She lifted her fingers from the keyboard of her typewriter. The invention itself was over a decade old. Her machine, however—the one extravagant purchase she'd made that year—still felt brand new. Anything that took her from it was of great annoyance.

Standing, she absentmindedly tucked one strand of hair behind her ear. Then she reconsidered and twisted the rest of her waist-length hair to form a loose knot at the base of her neck. It wasn't tidy, but it was better than going to the door all undone.

The wagon was obviously stopping outside her door, so she had no choice except to greet its passengers. Lord, she hoped no one wanted coffee. For that matter, she hoped no one wanted anything, as the kitchen was as bare of food as she was of hospitality and time for interruptions.

Crossing the worn yellow and blue rug, Charlotte automatically stepped over the small hole in the floorboard as she strode into the front hall. It was cluttered with her shoes, coat, umbrella, and various knickknacks. She took note of the comfortable mess with a slightly hopeless shrug.

When a sharp knock resounded from the other side of the door, startlingly loud in the silence, she froze. Then she took a deep breath.

"Coming." Charlotte hoped she didn't sound as irritated as she felt. No one respected other people's deadlines!

Yanking open the door, she nearly slammed it shut with surprise. Instead, she stepped back with a murmured, "Oh, my!"

Before her was a tall, dark-haired man with the most strikingly vivid blue eyes she'd ever seen. Astoundingly, he was dressed in a well-fitted suit of the neatest charcoal stripe. Out here, in the middle of nowhere!

However, what caused her extreme disconcertion was not his devilish good looks alone but rather the two young children standing on either side of him.

A young girl with two tidy blond braids was holding the man's hand and staring up at her intently. A little boy who had hair remarkably similar in color to Charlotte's own, shimmering with all the colors of autumn, and who barely came above the stranger's knee, clutched the man's tailored pant leg, causing a severe pucker.

"I understand this is the Sanborn homestead."

His voice, deep and pleasant, brought her attention back to him. She looked up dazedly, her own eyes blinking at the late spring sunlight behind him. Perhaps the whole apparition of handsome man and small children might simply disappear if she willed it.

"I am Charlotte Sanborn." Automatically, she stuck out her right hand to the stranger.

He looked at her hand, his face surprised.

"The writer?"

It was her turn for an expression of surprise, as a tremor of trepidation danced down her spine.

"How on earth . . . ?" she began. No one outside of Spring City knew that she was "Charles" Sanborn, the acclaimed writer, and she doubted even all of Spring knew or cared.

"Excuse me," he added, "I knew you were a woman, but I thought you would be older. That is, I'm delighted to meet you."

A genuine smile crossed his features for the first time, and taking her extended hand in his free one, he shook it with a firm grasp.

Charlotte felt a shock of warmth and strength, and realized it had been a long while since she'd touched someone else's skin.

"It is an honor and a pleasure," he continued. "I've read much of your work."

His voice was as warm as his hand, and she flushed.

Charlotte was used to praise, having been hailed as a voice of her time for the past few years by the editors with whom she had contact. She was successful in her own uncelebrated and quiet way, of course under the guise of her pseudonym.

However, knowing that this man had sat down with her work in his hands caused her to feel strangely exposed.

"Thank you," she said and stopped. She was waiting. He was waiting.

The children were waiting, too, but less patiently. The little boy tugged on the man's pant leg.

"Are we goin' in?" he asked, looking not at Charlotte but up at the tall man, who gave him a smile that stirred Charlotte's sentiment.

"Oh, I do apologize," she murmured, still thinking of the man's genuine smile. "Where are my manners?"

The little girl just stared at her as if she was wondering the very same thing, and Charlotte moved quickly aside to let them enter her home. She felt for all the world as if she had suddenly stepped out of her own life. A few moments ago, she could never have imagined a man and two children standing in her entryway.

"I am sorry to barge in on you, Miss Sanborn," he began, as his eyes took in the untidiness and the disrepair in one quick glance, "but after we arrived in Spring City, I discovered, of course, that there was no telephone system in place as yet."

They must be from the east, she concluded.

"I think it will be a while yet before those of us in Colorado have the benefits of Mr. Bell's invention." Having exhausted that topic, she waited again for him to explain himself.

"We hope you are not too inconvenienced, but we tried to be here as close to the appointed time as possible, barring a few mishaps along the way." This statement caused both the children to giggle, apparently having been the cause of some of the mishaps.

Charlotte frowned. "The appointed time, sir?"

"The trains were running late along the Topeka-Santa Fe line. A Pullman sleeper had overturned," he stated.

She nodded, finding nothing more to say, since the entire conversation so far was making no sense to her, and she usually prided herself on her quick understanding.

After a long moment, the man frowned. "Miss Sanborn, the children are tired. We stopped only briefly in Spring City to get directions, and I'm sure they would benefit from a short nap while we talk about their situation. Then, perhaps, some supper would be in order."

"Supper?" she repeated. The situation wasn't getting any better. Why would this family come to her house and demand a place to sleep and eat?

She pressed her hand to the side of her head. Having worked steadily for days to meet her editor's deadline, she was plum tuckered out. Charlotte was sure that was the reason none of this was coming clear to her.

"Miss Sanborn, is everything all right?" Even this tall, handsome stranger seemed a bit agitated now. His dark eyebrows formed the oddest pattern of straight and wavy lines as he frowned.

"Everything is just peart," she began, "except I must confess. I haven't the slightest idea who you are." She felt better for acknowledging the corn, as her neighbor called it.

It was the stranger's turn to flush. "How is that possible? I sent the letter myself."

"The letter?" At least this wasn't a random visit by lunatics wanting food. Perhaps soon she would get to the bottom of this, and she could return to her work.

"Yes," he affirmed. "Are you telling me that you never received correspondence from the offices of Malloy and Associates, posted about a month and a half past?"

"Malloy?" The name sounded familiar, but she couldn't place it.

"I've been awfully busy, Mr. . . . ah . . . ?"

"It's Malloy. Reed Malloy." He said it slowly as if speaking to a child, but his voice registered a tone of definite annoyance.

"You needn't get in a pucker, sir. I didn't realize you meant that you were—" but Charlotte broke off, deciding to ignore his tone.

"Let me take a look in my study. It's possible that something came and got overlooked. Editors forward a lot of mail from people who read my work. I don't always get a chance to look through it right away," she added apologetically.

Turning away, she entered her study, stepping delicately over the unsightly hole. The good Lord knew she often let papers and envelopes pile up. It was an unfortunate habit, and she would have to allow that it looked as if it had put her in some deep trouble now.

She heard them follow her, all three of them trailing behind, as she went to her desk and began to sift through the papers on the edge of it. When these finally slid to the floor, she bent to try another pile that already had collapsed off of a small oval Pembroke table, with its leaves always in the up position to accommodate more stray papers and books.

"It's amazing that your work, which seems to come from such an orderly mind, can be created here, in this chaos," observed the man behind her.

At his tone, she looked up. He seemed genuinely displeased, and she felt a little like a naughty school girl in front of the teacher. His sapphire eyes bore into hers for a second, and she felt the same jolt as when he had touched her hand.

She was the first to look away, continuing to rummage through the papers and then moving to a stack of Scientific American mixed with Yale Literary Magazine, ignoring his remark.

Charlotte wanted to tell him how she used to be organized, how she used to have food in the pantry and wood ready for the fires and not a speck of dust anywhere. She wanted to, but it would be a bald-faced lie. It had forever been this way—chaotic, at best. Her mind, however, was sharp and orderly and with it, she created works that were concise, easily understood, and a step ahead of her peers.

"Some of us have time to do housework," she commented lightly, "while others of us put our minds to more important things, such as . . . aha!"

"Did you salvage something, Miss Sanborn?"

She stood up and faced them, triumphantly waggling the cream-colored envelope with Malloy and Associates embossed in blue lettering on one side. "Here it is."

Charlotte recalled now having received it, even remarking over the blue ink and placing it on her desk to read after dinner, and then . . .

She stared guiltily at the dark-haired stranger with his flashing eyes. The seal had not even been broken.

"Perhaps you should open it and see why we're here," he continued evenly, crossing his arms over his broad chest, "although perhaps you could do that somewhere where we can all sit down. The children are growing tired."

"Of course." She had been caught out again without her best manners. Her mother would be appalled. While for the sake of Charlotte's father, her mother, Regina, had grown tolerant of the lack of societal niceties in the West, she had, nevertheless, tried to instill in her bookish daughter a sense of manners and the finer graces.

Charlotte was failing miserably on all counts, knowing in her heart this was why she welcomed her own isolation.

"Please, come this way." She passed between the boy and girl, who still stared at her as if she were a prize exhibit at the fair, and headed down the hallway to the parlor.

Tossing open the door, she froze. How long had it been since she'd used this room? It was dark and musty, and frankly, it smelled like a horse blanket.

"Excuse the state of the room. I don't entertain much. Let me just air it out a bit, but do come in and find a seat."

In the dark gloom, she could barely make out the furniture, all relics from her parents' day. She went directly over to the windows, pulling aside the heavy curtains, and opening the shutters, letting the fresh spring air flood the room, bringing with it the scent of the purple-flowered fireweed that grew all around the house.

Unfortunately, when she got to the third window, she opened the curtains and saw cracked panes of glass and a board nailed onto the sashes from the outside. Hastily drawing the curtain closed, she hoped the elegant man in her parlor had not noticed.

She turned to face her guests, who had spread themselves gingerly around the room. By the look on his face, it was undeniable that Mr. Malloy had seen the poor repair job. The little boy sat directly next to the man on the high-backed sofa in front of the rough stone fireplace with its faded, embroidered screen and an old rifle hanging above. The little girl had taken one of the moth-eaten, petit-point cushioned chairs that her mother had worked hard to create.

Charlotte was well aware of the dust still settling after they'd seated themselves. As she crossed the room, she noticed Reed Malloy's expression of disapproval. Inwardly mortified and feeling her stomach tense under the peculiarity of the situation, she sat in the only seat left, a small mauve-colored chair with bits of horsehair sticking out where it shouldn't be.

Taking the letter out of her skirt waistband, she opened it. Skimming the salutation and the niceties, suddenly she caught her breath.

"I take it you've reached the part where—" he began.

"Blazes!" Charlotte jumped out of her seat. "Ann gave the children to me? Is she mad? Does she understand—?"

"She is deceased, Miss Sanborn."

Charlotte sat down again slowly, her gaze darting to the children, who didn't seem to understand that the adults were speaking about their mother, Ann Connors. She turned her attention again to Reed Malloy, looking decidedly grave, his eyebrows once more in a fierce, straight line.

"Yes, I had heard, and I'm sorry. My aunt, Alicia, the children's grandmother, wrote to me about the tragedy."

Charlotte didn't bother to add that it was the sole time she'd heard from her aunt since her own parents had died nearly a decade earlier.

"You must understand, Mr. Malloy, I have never met my cousin, and we had only exchanged a few letters during the years. To say we were not close would be to put it mildly. My parents moved here from Boston before I was born." She paused, remembering what her aunt's letter described.

"It was a collision between my cousin's carriage and a horse car, as I recall. I know it is doubly hard with their father having died two years ago—"

"Three," Reed Malloy corrected, his glittering gaze never wavering.

"Three," she agreed, nodding. "In the light of this, I ask, why me as a guardian? Why not their grandmother?"

He stretched one arm out along the back of the sofa, glancing at each of the children, then his gaze fixed once more upon her.

"For one thing, their grandmother, your aunt, is nearly seventy years old. I don't believe your cousin thought that Alicia Randall would be an ideal mother."

Seventy! Charlotte hadn't known her mother's older sister was so much older.

"Secondly," he continued, "while you, Miss Sanborn, might not have given much thought to the eastern branch of your family, your cousin obviously gave a great deal of thought to you. Ann Connors had read all your work. In fact, it was she who first introduced me to your literary endeavors. She was one of your greatest admirers."

Charlotte felt as if she'd been socked in the stomach, and a lump rose into her throat at the thought of a cousin who knew so much about her when she, herself, hadn't even felt much grief at the announcement of her death . . . until now.

However, her life was set, and she liked it that way. She had no close friends, only acquaintances with whom she corresponded. Various editors checked in with her to assign an article or push her to keep a deadline. And she had one younger brother, Thaddeus, who popped up from time to time, making her miss him all the more when he went away again.

It was no life for children, and she was not the woman to raise them. How could she ever have imagined that her cousin would do such an absurd thing?

"It is simply out of the question, Mr. Malloy. I am profoundly sorry that you and the children wasted a trip. And I do apologize for not having opened your letter. I didn't recognize the seal and assumed it was a letter from a reader, which I would have looked at eventually."

She paused as she stood up, wondering if there was a way to seem less harsh but failing to think of one.

"However, and I do apologize again, but undoubtedly you can see that there is nothing I can do." As she finished, she spread her hands, giving a slight shrug.

Reed Malloy said nothing for a moment. His blue eyes merely narrowed at her. Then he stood up, dominating the room.

Charlotte held her breath a moment while he seemed to come to some decision. She waited for him to yell at her, grab the children, and burst from her house.

Instead, perfectly under control, he said, "It is I who am sorry, Miss Sanborn, but there is no choice here."

About to protest, she let out her breath in a rush, but he continued before she could speak a word.

"You have ample space, which was my main concern for a woman living alone, even if the house is in need of some repairs. As for your objections, you have made no valid ones, nor can make any as far as I can see."

"Really, Mr. Malloy—"

"Miss Sanborn, your young cousins will be no financial burden to you as their upbringing has been well-provided for. All you need offer them is shelter, basic human kindness, and a moral and intellectual example, which I believe you are capable of if I have read your works correctly. Can you not offer all of these?"

Of course she could! That was hardly the point. It was that no one had asked, and had someone done so, she would have said emphatically no. She had never had the desire to be a mother, nor had she any such desire now, not even when faced with the two sweet little urchins seated in her parlor. She refused to be bullied by his tactics.

"Mr. Malloy, neither my character nor my house is at issue."

He inclined his head slightly, acknowledging the way she had maneuvered out of that trap.

"Rather the question pertains to my inclination, which is strongly to the negative. I live a solitary life here." She gestured around her, taking in the house and the stretch of land outside her windows.

Her father had set up his homestead just a fifteen-minute walk outside of town, not too far from a mining camp in the foothills, yet far enough away from the bustle of Spring City that wagons weren't going by their window every minute, or even every day.

In recent years, the city bustled infrequently, only when miners came through discussing gold strikes or travelers mistook the area for one of the healing hot mineral springs. Spring City was down to one theater, for both opera and plays, and that was threatening to close any day now.

"There are no other children close by, though there is a school in town," she added thoughtfully, then bit her tongue before continuing. "Mr. Malloy, I am not a heartless individual. I wish the children no ill will."

She looked toward the two children now. Having comprehended that the adults were discussing where they were to live, they knew instinctively they weren't wanted, not by her. And they were no doubt relieved, Charlotte thought. They stood up, once more anchoring themselves to Reed Malloy, who absently stroked the top of the boy's head.

"Honestly," Charlotte rushed on, feeling like the hard-hearted cad she was professing not to be, "I simply want what's best for them, and that does not mean living here in a remote environment with a peace-and-quiet loving writer, who has absolutely no idea about raising children. Can you understand that?"

"At least we are in agreement that we both want what's best for the children," he said, as if he hadn't heard anything else she'd said. He glanced at each child, and Charlotte could see that he cared for them. Then his glance returned to her.

"And your suitability is a question in my mind. That's why I didn't blindly follow Ann Connors's last wishes, but accompanied them out here myself." He thought a moment. "Yes, if we're both worried about the same thing, then the answer seems obvious, wouldn't you agree?"

Charlotte began nodding even before she asked, "And what would that be?"

"Why, for me to stay here with you and the children, of course, to assess the situation. If I find that you are unacceptable after all, then I'll wire their grandmother, and we'll see if other arrangements can be made."

Seemingly satisfied with his pronouncement, he began to usher the children out of the room.

"Let's go, little ones, upstairs to your room. Auntie Charlotte will show you the way. Won't you?" He turned to her, the look on his face daring her to contradict his words in front of his tired wards.

Charlotte was still reeling from his highhanded manner, the way he seemed to treat her as if she were auditioning for a stage role. Unacceptable, indeed! Not to mention the unfamiliar address of "auntie," and the utterly improper suggestion that he should stay under the same roof with her.

Despite all that, after taking another look at the children's faces, she nodded again. Brushing past them, she headed for the stairs. She was sure she had said no, and very firmly, too. Yet somehow, all three of them seemed to be staying.

"Meanwhile," Reed Malloy continued, "I'll ride to town and wire my office that I shall be delayed indefinitely. Do you need me to pick up something for supper, Miss Sanborn?"

"Oh, yes," Charlotte said gratefully, forgetting for a moment that, if it weren't for him, she wouldn't need to be providing supper for anyone but herself. He was the source of all this confusion, yet she thought only of the empty cupboards and bare shelves in her pantry. Even her root cellar was rootless!

"Yes, whatever you and the children are accustomed to, Mr. Malloy."

Giving her a quick nod, he vacated her front hall. The infernal man seemed to be quite pleased with himself! To her sudden horror, Charlotte realized she was alone with the children and she didn't even know their names.

*End of Excerpt*

AN INTRIGUING PROPOSITION
PREQUEL

and the rest of the Defiant Hearts series
including

AN IMPROPER SITUATION
BOOK 1

AN IRRESISTIBLE TEMPTATION
BOOK 2

AN INESCAPABLE ATTRACTION
BOOK 3

AN INCONCEIVABLE DECEPTION
BOOK 4

AN IMPASSIONED REDEMPTION
NOVELLA

are available in print and ebook.

# ABOUT THE AUTHOR

*USA Today* bestselling author Sydney Jane Baily writes historical romance set in Victorian England, late 19th-century America, the Middle Ages, the Georgian era, and the Regency period. She believes in happily-ever-after stories with engaging characters and attention to period detail.

Born and raised in California, she has traveled the world, spending a lot of exceedingly happy time in the U.K. where her extended family resides, eating fish and chips, drinking shandies, and snacking on Maltesers and Cadbury bars. Sydney currently lives in New England with her family—human, canine, and feline.

You can learn more about her books, read her blog, sign up for her newsletter (and get a free book), and contact her via her website at SydneyJaneBaily.com. She loves to hear from her readers.

www.ingramcontent.com/pod-product-compliance
Lightning Source LLC
Chambersburg PA
CBHW031030190726
48286CB00003BA/1104